"You all right, *Tejano*? You sick, mebbe?"

A hand grabbed Slocum's hair and jerked his head upward. The general bent down and looked at Slocum with mock solicitude. "Don' worry, *Tejano*. You come to Mexico to see me, I give you somethin' to look at."

Slocum felt a wave of heat. For a moment he thought it was the sun, since it came from directly overhead.

Then he saw. It was a white-hot branding iron.

OTHER BOOKS BY JAKE LOGAN

RIDE, SLOCUM, RIDE
HANGING JUSTICE
SLOCUM AND THE WIDOW KATE
ACROSS THE RIO GRANDE
THE COMANCHE'S WOMAN
SLOCUM'S GOLD
BLOODY TRAIL TO TEXAS
NORTH TO DAKOTA
SLOCUM'S WOMAN
WHITE HELL
RIDE FOR REVENGE
OUTLAW BLOOD
MONTANA SHOWDOWN
SEE TEXAS AND DIE
IRON MUSTANG
SHOTGUNS FROM HELL
SLOCUM'S BLOOD
SLOCUM'S FIRE
SLOCUM'S REVENGE
SLOCUM'S HELL
SLOCUM'S GRAVE
DEAD MAN'S HAND
FIGHTING VENGEANCE
SLOCUM'S SLAUGHTER
ROUGHRIDER
SLOCUM'S RAGE
HELLFIRE
SLOCUM'S CODE
SLOCUM'S FLAG
SLOCUM'S RAID
SLOCUM'S RUN
BLAZING GUNS
SLOCUM'S GAMBLE
SLOCUM'S DEBT
SLOCUM AND THE MAD MAJOR
THE NECKTIE PARTY
THE CANYON BUNCH
SWAMP FOXES
LAW COMES TO COLD RAIN
SLOCUM'S DRIVE
JACKSON HOLE TROUBLE
SILVER CITY SHOOTOUT
SLOCUM AND THE LAW
APACHE SUNRISE

JAKE LOGAN
SLOCUM'S JUSTICE

BERKLEY BOOKS, NEW YORK

SLOCUM'S JUSTICE

A Berkley Book / published by arrangement with
the author

PRINTING HISTORY
Berkley edition / July 1983

All rights reserved.
Copyright © 1983 by Jake Logan.
This book may not be reproduced in whole or in part,
by mimeograph or any other means, without permission.
For information address: The Berkley Publishing Group,
200 Madison Avenue, New York, NY 10016.

ISBN: 0-425-06255-4

A BERKLEY BOOK® TM 757,375
Berkley Books are published by The Berkley Publishing Group,
200 Madison Avenue, New York, N.Y. 10016.
The name ''BERKLEY'' and the stylized ''B'' with design
are trademarks belonging to Berkley Publishing Corporation.

PRINTED IN THE UNITED STATES OF AMERICA

1

John Slocum put the twenty-four head of scrawny cattle across the dry arroyo and drove them up the bank to the level plain. Most of them stayed around the dry riverbed, pawing at the parched sand as if hoping that by some miracle water might suddenly well up.

It was too late in the summer for that. The sun struck at Slocum like a sword from beyond Rincón Mountain, and ropes of foam hung from the animals' mouths. They were in bad shape. They had had no water for three days. If he didn't find any for them soon, they would start to go blind. Slocum had filled his canteen with scummy green water three days before; it had the bite of harsh alkali, and it had made him sick, but it was water. He sat on his horse and watched his herd struggle wearily up the slope and stand there panting.

If they didn't drink that day they'd all be dead in the morning, and that would be the end of Slocum's attempt to start his own ranch along Paige Creek, east of Rincón Mountain, in the eastern part of Arizona.

He had bought the cattle with the slender proceeds from a bank holdup that went wrong. The man he had recruited to scoop up the money had lost control and fired into the silent group of clerks and customers without provocation, killing two men. One teller, enraged beyond self-preservation, had grabbed the man's gun right from his hand. Slocum had regretfully shot the man in the arm, scooped up whatever cash had been on the counter, and said crisply, "Let's move, you dumb son of a bitch!"

Four miles out of town Slocum reined in. "I go that way," he said. "You better go the other."

"Ain't we stickin' together?" the man whined. "I don't know this country."

"Ain't that just too bad," Slocum said. He reached into his saddlebag and pulled out twenty dollars.

"What the hell's that for?" his partner sputtered.

"Your help wasn't even worth that," Slocum said.

"You gimme half!"

In a conversational tone Slocum said, "Take this or take a bullet."

The man looked at Slocum's glittering green eyes and tightly compressed lips. He took the twenty and rode away.

The posse followed that man's trail and not Slocum's. But this was more than luck. Slocum had parted company with him at a dry arroyo with a granite floor. When he rode up the arroyo his horse left no hoofprints; the other man struck east on the dusty trail, and four hours later the posse caught up with him. One of the tellers was riding with the posse and identified him, and he was hanged immediately from a convenient cottonwood tree.

They didn't know whether he had buried the money somewhere or whether the other fellow had taken it. They backtracked until they found where the two tracks had separated. They followed the arroyo for four miles, hungry and thirsty. When Slocum, who was eating some beans and bacon on a ridge, saw them, he put down his plate and fired a warning shot with his

Winchester. The bullet richocheted off a flat rock and went screaming down the arroyo.

There was no place where the posse could hide. To move forward was suicide, to stay was suicide. To retreat was smart—but to retreat was to give up all hope of pursuit. Since they had one bank robber's corpse to their credit, they decided discretion was the better part of valor.

As they rode hastily away, Slocum grinned. He hated pointless killing. He sat cross-legged and scraped up the last of the beans with his old tablespoon as he watched them scramble down the arroyo. Then he emptied out his saddlebag and counted. There was $945. It was not much to balance against a double homicide charge plus bank robbery, and it was all that stupid bastard's fault. Slocum didn't yet know the man had been lynched. When he found out later, he nodded with satisfaction.

Slocum had bought the little ranch on Paige Creek three years earlier, under the name of Will Pearson. He bought the twenty-four head of two-year-old stock from the Day Ranch on Cienaga Creek for four hundred dollars. That was a lot of money, and he could have rustled them from another ranch if he had wanted to, but he wanted to be on good terms with his neighbors from the start. Besides, the cattle were in fine condition. Two years of good feeding and he would get forty dollars each for them from the wholesale butchers at Tucson—perhaps as much as fifty each if he sold them up at San Carlos to the agent for the Apaches.

Now that dream appeared to be going out the window. The thirsty cattle had already lost fifty or sixty pounds each in their long trek from the Day Ranch. The last time Slocum had come over the trail there had been plenty of water and plenty of grass, but that had been four years before. Unless they found some water soon, they would all die, and he would be back to the beginning in his attempt to start a new life.

As soon as the cattle scrambled up the ridge their heads jerked up. Tired as they were, they began trotting quickly in a northeasterly direction. They had smelled water. Slocum tried to remember what was there. Nothing, as far as he could recall, but he trusted their instincts, and he followed on his small but sturdy roan stallion, Six Bits. Four miles later he saw barbed wire. He galloped ahead. There was a clay water tank at the foot of a mountain, and it had gathered the spring runoffs. The water was a cool green and the grass around it grew tall and lush. In the middle of the barbed wire there was a gate with a padlock. Just outside the barbed wire, on the far side of the tank, was a little shanty with one small window in it. A crudely lettered sign was nailed to a fence post. It read, *No Trespassing. This Means You. You is Everyone except George Sheridan's Men.*

Clear enough, Slocum thought. But his cattle couldn't read. And there was no way he could break open the gate and let his cattle in. When they got close enough they would simply go through the wire; there was no way he could control the animals, crazed as they were by thirst. The wire would give them gashes which would be open avenues for infestation.

There was only one thing to do. Slocum took out his Colt and hammered out the staples which clenched the barbed wire to the fence posts. By the time his cattle came trotting up he had opened a space three fence posts wide. The cattle rushed in.

A few seconds later an old gray-bearded man came out of the shanty. His suspenders hung down over his thin shanks. He was drunk, but the double-barreled shotgun he pointed straight at Slocum's head did not waver a hair's breadth.

"Reach, you son of a bitch," he said. His voice was low, calm, and deadly.

Slocum reached.

2

The old man took an unsteady step closer.

"Get 'em the hell out," he said. His eyes were streaked with broken veins. He seemed to Slocum to be in his late seventies.

Slocum looked at the cattle. No one on earth could get them the hell out until they had drunk their fill.

"They got to have water," Slocum said soothingly.

"An' you knocked down the wire, di'n' yuh?"

"I wouldn't'a done it if I'd known you was here," Slocum said, still trying a placating tone. He wanted to prolong the parley until the cattle had drunk their fill. Then he intended to give the old man a gold double eagle, and chances were the old codger would be so happy that he would forget the whole thing.

"Think I'm stupid, you young whippersnapper?" The old eyes measured Slocum. There was no mercy there, no weakness. This man would not take a double eagle and forget the whole thing, Slocum realized. The old man moved closer, staggering a bit, leaning against the fence posts for support as he neared.

"Oughta kill yuh," he said calmly. "Knockin' down the fence 'n' all. Trespassin' on this yere property. I don' give a rebel damn 'bout your scrawny culls, an' neither does George Sheridan. Now git."

Slocum didn't like the fact that the old man didn't holler. Yelling would let him blow off steam, and then

6

he might calm down and listen to reason. By keeping so quiet he was keeping his rage at a rolling boil. He would be very hard to talk out of anything. More than a double eagle was indicated, Slocum decided.

"I'll pay you for the water," Slocum said, and turned toward his saddlebag.

"Keep your hands on the pommel, boy."

The old man brought up the muzzle sharply. It wavered a bit, but always within the drunken oscillations was Slocum's groin or belly or chest. The old man was clearly allowing for his drunken condition in case he decided to fire. Slocum's stomach felt ice-cold.

"I got money in my saddlebag," he said. "You just take it. I'll keep my hands on the pommel, all right."

The old man moved closer, touching an occasional fence post for support. "Don' want your cattle to piss in my water, son," he said. "I don' want your goddamn money, neither. George'll take my haid off when he sees them hoofmarks and that downed fence."

"I got sixty bucks in the saddlebag," Slocum said, as calmly as he could. He knew he was very close to dying.

"Don' turn your hoss, son. Stay on this yere side of 'im."

He was ten feet away. Slocum knew the old man wanted to get in back of him. He was going to be shot in the back, and to hell with honor. The old man was a hard bastard, and he had probably survived this long by breaking all the rules.

"Sixty-five bucks, free and clear," Slocum offered.

"Free 'n' clear, your ass. Geroge is m' nephew, boy. He'll be down on me like the hull goddamn Missouri on a sandbar. He'll be by at supper time fer a look-see. I'm nothin' but a pore ol' man, ol' enough to be your granddaddy, 'n' yuh want me t' ketch hell? He'll eat me raw without salt fer not shootin' yuh. Yuh trespassed, yuh destroyed his property, 'n' now yer offerin' a bribe? That's 'nough talkin'. Git down."

"I'll pay eighty-five bucks." That was all Slocum had in the saddlebag, all that was left.

"I'm done talkin', son," the old man said heavily. The two barrels jerked as he cocked the shotgun. At the dry, ominous sound, Slocum's horse flicked his ears sideways.

"You use that thing," Slocum said casually and slowly, "you'll hang."

"Damn fool kid!" the old man chortled. "Sheriff's George Sheridan's nephew. George *owns* Saguaro County: cows, fences, water, jails, gen'ral store, 'n' cemetery. Git down. My side." He moved along the barbed wire toward Slocum.

His suspenders caught in the wire, and he looked down for a second to free them. Slocum grabbed this chance. He threw himself out of the saddle and pulled his Colt as he did so. As the old man swung the muzzle of the shotgun up and pulled both triggers, Slocum fired. There was no time for him to risk his life by trying for an arm. The old man went down with a blue hole in his forehead. Six Bits screamed as the blast blew away his right foreleg.

Slocum put his second shot into Six Bits' brain. He thrashed once, then lay still. Slocum felt more regret for his horse than for the old man. The old man's suspenders were tangled onto the fence even more by his fall. His skinny behind was uppermost, the tobacco-stained mouth pressed into the dust. The bloodshot eyes glared blindly. Several of the cattle, their thirst slaked, lifted their heads and stared at the two dead creatures.

Water dripped off their muzzles. Satisfied, they lowered their heads and continued to drink.

Slocum thought fast. The mountains were twenty-five miles to the east. There he could lose his trackers. The mountains were full of canyons, hidden springs, shade, and shelter. There were still renegade Apaches there, but Slocum would rather deal with them than with this Sheridan and his men, bent on vengeance.

Slocum's cattle had his road brand on them. That, and his own brand, were registered in the county seat. The horse had the same brand on him. *Jesus Christ,* Slocum thought, *I might as well take a full-page advertisement in the Flagstaff paper saying I did it.*

He had paid eighty dollars for that custom-made saddle up in Flagstaff. He shot the fattest steer—not that there was much choice in that starved, exhausted lot—and cut off several steaks to bring with him. He filled his canteen with some of Sheridan's fresh water and slung his saddlebags over his shoulder, then paused for a moment to think over his plan.

He could work south along the ridges in the mountains, the way the Apaches moved when they didn't want to be noticed on their raids into Mexico. In five or six days he would cross the border. He didn't want to attract attention by shooting game, but the meat should keep him going until he got into Mexico. He would have to stay out of sight of anyone who might mention to Sheridan a single man hoofing it south. There would be an occasional lone miner up there in the mountains— maybe a small rancher, like he had been only ten minutes before.

Slocum laughed, then shrugged. Life was a seesaw. He could just forget about his little spread. And he would have to walk in his stockinged feet to the mountains; walking in his boots that distance would raise crippling blisters before he went five miles. He would have to move fast; the old man had said Sheridan would be along that afternoon. Maybe he could buy a horse when he got past the border. No Mexican gave a damn what a gringo was doing, as long as he had money. North of the border, there were too many curious people.

By nightfall, Slocum had reached the foothills. His feet were a mess: torn, bleeding, full of cactus thorns, bruised by pebbles.

He dropped and fell asleep immediately. It was cold, but he was so tired he didn't care. At sunrise he stood up and found a dry streambed. It was easier going there, stepping from flat stone to flat stone. He stopped and ate some hardtack and drank some of the water out of his canteen. He hadn't found any more fresh water in the mountains. The hardtack was soaked from the raw, bloody steaks, but he had eaten worse meals in the Confederate Army. He didn't risk making a fire yet. If he found some buffalo chips, or something else that wouldn't make any smoke, he could make a little palm-sized fire and cook a steak. He unscrewed his canteen, threw his head back, and saw, far below across the grasslands, just about where the old man lay over the barbed wire, a big dust. He screwed the cap back on the canteen and kept moving.

3

Slocum spent the night in a small hollow at the crest of one of the mountains. He had never felt so tired in his life. It was the second night he had to spend without a blanket, but again he was so exhausted that it meant nothing. The side of the hill was covered with loose pebbles. An Apache might be able to climb up during the night without starting a small and noisy landslide, but nobody else could.

Slocum's feet were even more blistered than before, and covered with cuts and bruises. As soon as there was enough light he made a tiny fire, Indian fashion, and cooked one of the steaks. He was afraid that even those few tiny wisps of smoke might attract unfriendly attention from the pursuers, so he kicked the fire out and ate the steak almost raw. When he lifted his canteen for a drink it was empty, but he remembered noticing a narrow reed-bordered creek at the foot of the hill.

Wary as always, Slocum did not stand up and walk down to the water. He took off his sombrero and slowly raised his head behind a clump of mesquite clustered on the rim of his little hollow.

In the middle of the creek a Chiricahua Apache, wearing a necklace of polished mussel shells, sat astride a scrawny cow pony. The water came up to the horse's belly. As the horse drank, the Apache idly swung a foot back and forth, splashing the water, yawning, and stretching as he watched the other members of his war party washing and drinking in the creek. The sun had not yet turned the atmosphere into a blazing hell; it was the best part of the day. The sun was warm, but a cool breeze was blowing down off the crest.

Another Apache, sitting his horse nearby, noticed a few broken reeds where Slocum had passed the night before. He dismounted and followed the trail. He was only faintly curious, and what saved Slocum was that he had gone without his boots. His feet made a moccasin-like trail. The Apache who was watering his horse called out to the tracker in an irritated manner, but the man was still interested in finding out what kind of an Indian had been there.

Slocum eased his Colt out of the holster. There were eleven men in the party. At the first shot, the rest would scatter like quail and melt into the chaparral like smoke. Three of them had carbines. They would be sure to encircle him and come down at him from the top of the bowl in which he was lying. He eased back the hammer and waited.

The Apache parted the reeds in front of him with his long lance. Slocum saw him stop suddenly. A big female rattler had slithered out and lay coiled in his path, rattling vigorously. Several baby rattlers were sprawled near her. The Apache leaped backward so quickly that he stumbled and fell back into the creek. The others saw what had happened and they all laughed at their comrade's discomfiture. Then they mounted and rode to the south.

Slocum waited half an hour. He moved downhill and gave a wide berth to the mother rattler, even though he couldn't see her any more. He filled his canteen and climbed quickly to the ridge opposite. As soon as he reached the top he saw some crude timberwork halfway up the ocotillo-covered slope. It was the top of a one-man mine shaft. Next to it was a small corral with a horse and a mule in it. Beyond that stood a small, ramshackle shanty with one tiny window; glass was too fragile to be transported out here.

The door was open. When Slocum reached it he saw a dirty miner in a checked woolen shirt frying bacon. His back was to the door. He wore a gun belt with a long-barreled Remington Frontier .44. It had a custom-made cherry wood grip.

"Don't turn around," Slocum said softly, "or I'll have to kill you."

The man froze.

"Now, you just set the pan on the stove, unbuckle your gun, and let the whole shebang drop."

"Cartridge in the chamber," the man said grumpily but without fear. "Might go off."

"Then just set it down nice and easy instead."

The man set the gun down gently.

"Don't look around just yet, friend. Kick it backward towards me. Easy does it, mister." The man obeyed, and Slocum shoved the gun into his belt. "Where's the rifle?" he asked.

"No rifle. Got a carbine," the miner said, still in the same grumpy, unconcerned tone that told Slocum that he had seen everything and that this was just another little setback in the life of a solitary miner in Arizona.

He pointed backwards, still not turning around. The carbine lay across a deer's antlers which had been nailed above the door. Slocum pulled it down and looked at it. It was a Winchester .44 with a brass-covered action. He cradled it in his left arm.

"Whaddya want, mister? I ain't got no money, I ain't got no bags o' dust buried here. If I did I sure wouldn't stick 'round *here*."

"I want to buy your horse."

"You gotta stick a gun in my back to buy a horse?"

"Shows I'm serious. How much?"

"I don't wanna sell 'er."

"Turn around."

The miner did so. He saw a tall man wearing worn rancher's clothes. Green eyes blazed out of his hard tanned face.

"Once more," Slocum said quietly, "how much?"

"Seventy-five."

"She's so swaybacked my feet'll drag. Forty."

"I ain't bargainin', mister. It's my only horse if I wanna get outta here in a hurry. You want 'er, seventy-five."

"And the saddle?"

"I got a Mex saddle hung over the bobwire back of the shanty. It set me back eighty-five when I was ranchin'."

"You used both of 'em plenty. I'll give you eighty-five for both of 'em, with a saddle blanket thrown in."

"Nope."

"Eighty-five is all I got, friend." Slocum cocked the Colt.

"We got a deal," said the miner. He was a realist.

Slocum emptied his saddlebag on the floor, counted out the eighty-five, and shoved everything else back.

"I saw some Apaches this morning along the creek," he said. "I'll leave your carbine and Colt a couple miles south. Don't want to leave 'em here. You might get to feeling cocky soon's I leave."

"Thanks, but that's no news 'bout 'paches. Them

buggers go up 'n' down the valley stealin' horses 'n' sellin' 'em down in Mexico, stealin' 'em in Mexico 'n' sellin' 'em back up here. I leave 'em alone, they leave me alone. We got a sort of agreement. You in trouble with Mr. George Sheridan?''

"Now what makes you think that?" Slocum asked. He picked up a pair of boots. They were too small.

"No 'fense meant, but that's a right foolish question. You're headin' fer Mexico like a bat outta hell. Might's well save yourself the trouble, mister.''

"What's this Sheridan like?"

"Well, he ain't so bad 'cept when he's drunk. He gits drunk often 'n' stays drunk long. When he's sober he's just as mean, 'n' he's sober whenever he ain't drunk. When he's sober he jus' lays there like a rattler 'n' waits fer you to walk by. But he ain't no gentleman, 'cause he don't rattle. Son of a bitch, that must be the chink where the wind come in last winter 'n' gimme such a crick in the back o' my neck. I hadda get some hoss liniment 'n' tear up my ol' red skivvies—''

For the first time he noticed Slocum's bleeding feet. He whistled.

"Had a run-in with Mr. Sheridan oncet," he said. "I had a little spread by the Rio Guajalote. He was jus' beginnin' t' feel his oats. His cows were all havin' twins or triplets while my cows 'n' my neighbors' cows were all pretty much barren. He hadn't put his bobwire in yit, so my cows would hang 'round Sheridan's corrals, full o' envy for his cows' children, 'n' bawlin' 'cause they di'n't have none. I talked it over with three other small ranchers like I was, out along the Guajalote, 'n' we wuz obliged to call 'round thataway. We threatened to hang 'im, to hell with the law, if his cows had any more twins. You see the result of that little talk? I'm runnin' this goddamn shaft alone.''

''What happened?''

''Lemme give you some iodine, son. You c'n take it with you. Out o' them four ranchers, I'm the only one alive today. An' he took all our property. I had a son. He died full o' 'pache arrers. It was Sheridan's nephew, Joe Hannum, who found 'im. I went up where Joe said he found m' boy. All the hoss tracks 'round was made with iron horseshoes. Hell, you know 'paches ain't got shod horses. I found a couple cigarette butts, two empty pint whiskey bottles, plenty boot marks. No moccasin tracks anywheres. I'm alive 'cause I'm yaller. He made me an offer for peanuts 'n' I sold out. The others jus' died. One in Dodge City, accidental in his hotel room. He was lookin' up the barrel of his Colt while cleanin' it and it went off. George Sheridan was in the next room, 'n' he testified at the inquest. Said he was talkin' with Woodhouse while Woodhouse was cleanin' the gun, and Woodhouse was drinkin' 'n' had the shells in it, 'n' was spinnin' the cylinder. Sheridan said he got the hell out, Woodhouse bein' so careless 'n' all.

''Then Sheppard died from a broken neck. He ran 'gainst a low tree branch in the dark, ridin' home. He rode that road for over twenty years, 'n' he knew every foot of it. He passed by a saloon where Sheridan's men used to hang out. They found 'im under a tree, they said. Dumped him 'crost his own saddle 'n' brung 'im to the sheriff. The sheriff is 'nother Sheridan nephew, Sam Hannum. Sam said it was death by misadventure.

''Sheppard's daughter lived back East. Sheridan made

'er an offer—peanuts again. But no one else dared make a bid, so she sold it to him. So lemme give you some advice, son. I don' know what you did that makes you take off in your stockin' feet. Mebbe spit on the floor of a saloon, mebbe raided a watermelon patch. Change your name right away, 'n' don't stop soon's you cross the border t' git a job in one o' those big Mex ranches. Jus' keep goin'. I wouldn't stop till I got past Durango.''

Slocum nodded. "So long," he said. He threw his saddlebag over his shoulder.

"You got real big feet, mister. Wish I had boots 'd fit you. But at least you c'n ride till you find a pair."

Slocum turned towards the door.

"Enjoyed your visit. Don't git chances t' talk much up here. Effen you'd like to set awhile I'll make a big mess o' bacon 'n' eggs."

"Got to get moving. Thanks anyway."

"Jus' stick m' artillery somewhere in the shade. Shore would hate t' burn m' hands on 'em, friend."

The miner followed Slocum outside and watched him sling an old saddle blanket over the horse and proceed to saddle and bridle the old horse.

"No trouble t' make a mite extry," the miner pleaded. "I make good biscuits."

Slocum shook his head and rode away. He wanted to put plenty of distance between Sheridan and himself, especially after what he had just heard. The little horse was out of condition and resented being forced to move at a pace faster than a slow amble. Without spurs, the horse was unheeding when Slocum raked him with his bare heels. He tried to graze wherever there was grass, and long before Slocum found a shady place to set down the miner's guns, he had cracked open the horse's mouth with his irritated jerking at the bit.

It took an hour more for the horse to learn that his rider was even more stubborn than he was. Once that was settled, the horse got down to a steady pace, and Slocum pushed him until it was too dark to see.

4

Three days later and fifty miles into Sonora Slocum woke up suddenly. A scuffed boot toe was prodding him viciously in the small of his back.

His horse had broken a leg scrambling down a rocky slope the day before. Still without boots, he had walked on for seven hours, his saddlebags slung over his shoulder. He had found a woodcutter's hut and had fallen asleep in it. During the early hours of the morning, while he was deep in exhausted sleep, a sudden thunderstorm had sprung up. There was no other way the strange men standing over him could have come close without Slocum's hearing them.

His hand shot under the saddlebag he was using for a pillow, but the Colt was gone. Standing over him were four men, wearing dripping yellow saddle slickers. The man who had prodded him awake loomed over Slocum. He was tall and fat, and as he pulled the slicker off Slocum saw the sheriff's star. The sheriff's stomach bulged far over his gun belt. He stank of sweat and hard riding.

"S'pose he's the one?" asked the sheriff.

One of the men squatted on his heels. He pulled back his slicker and revealed a gray flannel shirt. He unbuttoned a pocket and pulled out a creased, stained telegram. It was a long message, and Slocum could read the signature:

J. RODMAN, COUNTY CLERK, TUCSON, ARIZONA TERRITORY

"Lessee now," the man said. "In re— in response to your telegram of fifty inst— what the hell's *that* mean?"

"Jesus," said the sheriff heavily, "gimme."

Slocum figured the sheriff for Sam Hannum, Sheridan's nephew. The sheriff read rapidly and easily, looking at Slocum from time to time. " 'William Pearson, owner of Bar W brand, registered three years ago, about thirty-seven, about five feet ten, black hair, green eyes, scar across back of left hand—' "

The man who had squatted let out a triumphant rebel yell. "That's him! That's him, all right!"

The sheriff folded the telegram carefully and replaced it in the man's pocket. He buttoned the pocket carefully. Slocum could see that Hannum was a methodical man.

"All right," he said, turning to Slocum, "I arrest you fer the murder of Jacob Waterman. Get on your horse."

"You can't arrest me in Mexico, you damn fool," Slocum said. "Besides, I don't have a horse." He knew he was not being realistic. He was very careful not to make any sudden moves.

"Don't worry 'bout that. We brought an extry one along just in case. Get up 'n' strip."

Slocum stood up and stripped, tossing each article of clothing to the sheriff as he did so. Hannum went through the pockets. Then the man saw that Slocum did not wear a money belt. He bent down, emptied the saddlebags, and kicked through the contents in disgust. "Broke?"

Slocum said nothing.

"Dress," Hannum said. "What happened to your boots?"

Slocum said nothing. Hannum swung a backhanded slap that knocked Slocum across the room. He came up lightly as a cat to his feet, hands outstretched. But two guns were pointed at him. He slowly dropped his hands. He would wait until the chances were better.

They tied his hands to the pommel. His ankles were linked by a short length of rope running under the horse's belly.

"You're lucky, Pearson," the sheriff said. "If I had my way, I'd leave yuh to a couple 'paches. Let 'em spread-eagle yuh down on the flats an' let them women work yuh over. An' what are we gonna do instead? Set yuh on a horse under a cottonwood, 'n' slap 'im in the ass. Less'n a minute is all it takes. You're lucky George Sheridan is civilized. Let's mosey on."

During the three days it took them to get back, Slocum did not say a word. He couldn't bribe them with money or promises of money; they knew he was broke, a small rancher working a tiny spread. Nor could he claim protection from any of the sheriffs or marshals in the hot little cow towns through which he rode, bareheaded and barefoot, while kids raced alongside yelling, "What's he done, mister?"

Huge blisters formed at the back of his neck. The sun seemed to grow enormous at noon, until the whole sky burned like a blast furnace. They gave him hardly any water. It was a blessing in a way, because all he could think about was water, and his ultimate execution meant less and less to him. His captors tried to tease him by deliberately spilling water from their canteens whenever they drank. Once Sam Hannum hurled water onto Slocum's face while his eyes were closed against the sun's glare. Startled, Slocum opened his eyes and licked the few drops that had remained on his lips. He enjoyed fantasies of revenge in which Hannum begged for water and Slocum poured melted silver down his throat while saying to Hannum, "How's this for money, you son of a bitch?"

On the last morning Hannum lit five fires in a row and threw damp weeds on them when they were burning strongly. Five columns of thick gray smoke rose straight up in the still air. It was an Indian sign, and Slocum knew what it meant: five men were returning, although four went out.

Hannum turned to Slocum. "Sheridan's gonna git some real estate ready fer yuh. You're gonna be a permanent trespasser, an' it ain't gonna cost yuh a cent." He grinned.

Slocum looked at him without expression. He had been in tough situations before, but this one looked hopeless. One thing was sure: they thought he was going to plead for his life. But one other thing was even more sure: he had been a Southern officer in the Civil War, and he intended to die with honor.

His face was burned raw under a week's growth of beard. One of the blisters on the back of his neck had broken. His bare feet were raw and puffy where cactus spines had penetrated and become infected. His tongue had swollen until it almost filled his mouth.

The windmill by the water tank was motionless. On the fence sat several buzzards, their wings spread in the still, hot air. The fence had been repaired, Slocum noticed. The buzzards sidled slightly as the men rode by, their snake-like necks twisting to watch. Back of the shanty lay the rib cage of Six Bits. It had been picked clean by the buzzards. Slocum turned his face away.

"I ast could I kill yuh when I caught up with yuh," Hannum said, riding alongside Slocum. "Sheridan said no. Said he wanted everything real legal. Said he wanted to see yuh alive." He opened his jackknife and leaned over to cut the rope tying Slocum's ankles together. Then he untied Slocum's hands from the pommel and handcuffed them in front. Suddenly he gave Slocum a vicious, abrupt shove. Slocum fell and landed on his blistered face in the dust. He made no sound. He did not believe in wasting energy uselessly. He saved everything he had for the one critical moment in which he might need every particle of energy.

"Git up."

Slocum struggled to his knees, then stood erect painfully.

"He said alive, so he'll git yuh alive. But not by much," Hannum said with a grin on his pudgy face. "We're gonna cover the last five miles in style. But yuh ain't gonna like me."

He shook out twenty feet of his riata and tied one end to the handcuff chain. Then he swung his horse around and headed for the ranch house at a fast walk. After fifteen feet Slocum stumbled over a clump of sagebrush. His sunburned face plowed through the pebbled desert floor. Hannum jerked him erect and pulled. After Slocum fell several times, Hannum slowed his pace regretfully. After forty-five minutes of this, with an occasional stumble, Slocum's feet felt like two large overstuffed pillows filled with feathers. They were inefficient for walking or for supporting him upright. They could hold him up for a few feet at a time until Hannum impatiently jerked his riata. Then down he went again.

One of the men said, "Goddlemighty, Sam, he looks like an ol' sun-dried bucket about to fall to pieces." Another man added, "He don't stand no more show than a stump-tailed bull in fly time."

Slocum was panting like a dog as he stumbled and floundered through an ocean of chaparral. He was covered with gray dust.

The little group moved to the top of a hill and halted.

Below them lay George Sheridan's ranch house. It was an adobe fortress built around a huge patio in which grew several live oaks and two old cottonwoods. High up around the upper rim of the adobe there were rifle slits. At the corner closest to Madrona Creek, the little river that flowed through the bottom of the valley, rose a forty-foot watchtower. It also had rifle slits. Several saddled horses were grazing among the twisted and trampled sunflowers that filled the space between the house and the Madrona. From the crests of the hills surrounding the valley, green meadows ran clear down to the river. The whole formed a lush, well watered green saucer.

Halfway down the hill on which they were standing was a little cemetery. A freshly filled grave lay at one end. Next to it was a grave that had been dug a few hours before, as Slocum could tell by the damp root fibers that lay exposed in the freshly turned soil.

Hannum grunted with satisfaction. "They got my message all right," he said with satisfaction. Slocum's breath was coming in great, heaving gasps that whistled as his chest labored. The salty sweat running into his eyes made them smart. He lifted his handcuffed wrists in order to wipe them, and Hannum jerked the rope hard. Slocum fell headlong.

"The grave looks a mite small, don't it, Mr. Pearson?

But yuh won't mind my doublin' yuh up. I'm sure o' that.''

For the first time in three days Slocum spoke. His tongue was so thick that it was hard to make it work.

''You'd have enough guts for that,'' he said.

Hannum flushed and the other two men snickered. Hannum jerked Slocum violently to his feet. As he was jerked past the cemetery he noticed that most of the markers were plain wooden slabs. Almost all marked the graves of cowpunchers who had been killed by Apaches, by gunshot, or by a horse. One marker, carved more carefully than the rest, said simply:

MARY MCDOWELL SHERIDAN 1849–1875

Next to it was a tall marble shaft that said:

GEORGE SHERIDAN, JR. July 1, 1875–August 10, 1881
CHILDREN ARE AN HERITAGE OF THE LORD.

Hannum spurred his horse to a trot. As Slocum was dragged and jerked for the last five hundred yards, one savage thought burned inside his skull: he had to get his hands on a gun. He could handle one even with the handcuffs on. The only thing he was afraid of was that Hannum had rammed the cuffs on so tightly that his numbed fingers might not have accurate control once he got his hands on a gun. But that was a risk he would have to take.

5

As Slocum's eyes adjusted to the dim light inside the ranch house he heard a slow, creaking noise. The sound came from a long, cylindrical mass that moved back and forth. Several parallel bars of light on the wall opposite him got their shape from the sun pouring in through the rifle slits high up in the walls. The hard oak floor felt cool to the bloody, torn soles of his feet.

When his eyes became adjusted to the dimness he saw that the dark mass swinging slowly back and forth was a Yucatan hammock suspended from two of the oak beams that supported the roof. From a nail driven into one of the beams hung a fully loaded gun belt with a .45 in it. By the deference showed toward the hammock by the men in the huge, dim room, Slocum knew that George Sheridan, the owner of the Big S, was resting in it. As he watched, filled with curiosity in spite of pain and thirst, a spurred boot came out of the hammock and kicked at the floor. The hammock began to sway more quickly. The boot stayed out of the hammock, balanced lightly on the rowel of its spur. The rowel rolled back and forth as the hammock swung. Seeing all the old, deep scratches on the floor, Slocum knew that this must be a habit of Sheridan's.

A calm, deep voice growled something. Hannum promptly dug out a match and lit the long cigar George Sheridan was holding in his mouth. His hand was big and brown, and a plain, wide gold wedding band was on the ring finger. The little finger next to it was missing; it had been blasted off in a gunfight, Slocum learned later. A cloud of fragrant smoke drifted upward as George Sheridan clasped his hands behind his neck and stared at Slocum.

Sheridan was clean-shaven and had big shoulders. He and Slocum were both big, powerful men, but Sheridan was taller. Slocum judged the man to be in his early fifties. He wore a clean white linen shirt buttoned carefully to the top, which was held with a little gold stud on which was engraved a tiny rose. His face was in shadow.

Slocum looked around the room. The men beside him stood silently, waiting for Sheridan to speak. The room was a hundred feet long and twenty-five feet wide, Slocum judged. Several couches covered with buffalo robes and Navajo blankets stood along the walls. Men were sprawled on the couches staring at Slocum. There were eight transverse roof beams, hand-hewn a thousand years ago. Sheridan had them taken out of the cave dwellings in the upper Navajo country five hundred miles to the north and had them freighted south when he built the ranch house. From each roof beam hung a bronze lamp holding a gallon of kerosene. On either side of the massive oak door were carbine racks containing fifteen Winchesters each.

"Had a good look?" asked Hannum. "Didja git a good look at the wagons outside?"

Slocum paid no attention. He looked at the ladder going up to the tower. There was a floor high up in the tower, and the rifle slits. By craning his neck he could see boxes of ammunition neatly stacked beside each slit. He lowered his gaze. In one corner of the huge room were sacks of potatoes, dried beans, onion, dried beef, and what looked like barrels of water and kegs of bourbon. The place was a fortress, built to withstand a long siege in high comfort.

Slocum had seen the wagons, and he knew what they were for. They were to hang him. Two of the wagons had been lashed together by their front wheels to keep them from separating. The wagon tongues were also lashed together and were pointing straight up. They were used to hang men when there was no tree available. But there was a big cottonwood outside in the patio. It had a good, strong horizontal branch fourteen feet above the ground. It was ideal for a hanging, and Slocum wondered why they had bothered with the wagons. He heard one of the men whisper behind him, "How come he ain't usin' that puffeckly good cottonwood?"

"Ever since his boy died," the other man whispered in reply, "he don't use that tree none."

"How come? Don't make no sense."

"That there ol' branch is where the boy used to hang his swing."

"Ah," said the other man respectfully.

"Las' time we hung someone," Hannum said in Slocum's ear, "we let 'im hang there fer a week. Coulda sworn the man's neck was three feet long. You—"

Sheridan's hand went up slightly, palm out. Hannum stopped talking as if the big square palm had been clapped over his mouth.

Sheridan asked, "Why didja kill the old man?" The voice was soft and pleasant.

Slocum said, "I asked him for water for my cattle. He wouldn't give me any or sell me any. He got madder and madder and he pulled down on me with that shotgun and I could see he was going to use it. He was slower than I was.''

"Don't gimme that!" said Hannum.

"You want to know the real reason?" asked Slocum.

The silence was so profound that Slocum felt it could be cut with a knife.

"Yeah?" asked Hannum.

"He smelled bad," Slocum said. He spoke with difficulty.

Much to his surprise, a low, amused rumble came from the hammock. It shook a little and subsided. The other boot swung into view and George Sheridan finally sat up, swung around, stretched the hammock with his arms, then leaned back.

"And *dumb!*" Sheridan said. "A man with a double-barreled shotgun lettin' hisself get kilt by a li'l ol' Colt. Why, that's shameful. I'm real sorry to be kin to him." He blew some smoke at the ceiling. *"Dumb!"* he repeated with vehemence, slapping his thigh. "Take off his handcuffs. Someone bring 'im some water. I wanna hear what he has t' say."

Hannum reluctantly dug a key out of his pocket. Slocum's wrists had puffed out so much over the tight metal bands that the sheriff had trouble inserting the key. No one made a move to give Slocum any water. Slocum looked at his hands. The wrists looked like gigantic red sausages.

Near Slocum a lean youngster lounged on one of the buffalo-covered couches. He had been one of Slocum's captors. His name was Eddie. His feet were thrust out in front of him. One spur rested on the floor, and one boot heel was locked into the instep of the other boot. He emitted a horrible, tuneless whistling. His sombrero was pushed down over his nose.

"Eddie!" Sheridan called sharply.

Eddie got up resentfully and dipped a tin cup into a large clay olla hanging from a hook. Slocum's legs were trembling from that last painful dragging through the mesquite. He was forcing them to remain rigid lest anyone think he was losing control. Three feet away from Slocum stood Sam Hannum, with his thumbs hooked into his gun belt. A level bar of sunlight cut across his bulging belly. For the first time Slocum noticed that the butt of the .45 hanging from the nail was made of a black material that looked to him like ebony. Spades, hearts, diamonds, and clubs had been cut out of silver and inlaid in the black butt.

Eddie walked across with a cup of water: Slocum knew that Eddie would have liked very much to throw it at him. Even though it hurt his raw, burned face, he grinned as he took the cup. He needed both hands to hold it. With great difficulty his fingers obeyed his wish to close around the cup.

"Think you're the king bee, don't'cha?" Eddie said. He looked down at Slocum's wrecked feet. "Yuh like the li'l walk we took?" He laughed.

Slocum took several small sips. It would not do to put a lot of water into his dehydrated belly at once. He soaked his tongue in each mouthful before he swallowed. It was better than the best whiskey he had ever drunk. Then he said critically, "Woulda enjoyed it more if you were prettier."

Sheridan roared with laughter and slapped his boot. "All right," he finally said, "Eddie, sit down. Y'asked fer it 'n' yuh got it." He inhaled deeply on his cigar and blew the smoke gently up. The fragrant blue mist drifted among the festoons of dried red peppers hanging from the oak beams. Slocum watched the smoke eddy in and out of the peppers as Eddie, muttering, settled himself again on the buffalo robe. Slocum kept working his fingers, trying to encourage the circulation. If he were to make any kind of move, those fingers had better be in decent working condition.

"I'd hate like hell to be shut up in a winter line camp with you off somewheres," Sheridan said, staring at Eddie. "I shore would." He sighed and turned in the hammock. "All right, Mr. Pearson, you wanted my water bad, 'n' now you're gonna pay for it. But we're gonna have a jury trial, first off. Don' look so surprised. I respect the law. Get the good book, Eddie."

Eddie untwisted his scuffed boots and in his sullen fashion picked up a small Bible from a heavy walnut oak table that stood in a dark corner.

"Fust thing we gotta do," Sheridan said, "is swear in a jury. Swear in a jury, Sheriff."

Sam Hannum counted the men in the room. There were eight. He stepped outside and brought in four of the men who had been squatting outside in the shade of the ranch house. They took off their hats while an old white-haired man began to swear them in.

"I don't think this is going to be legal," Slocum said.

The old man stopped and stared at him. He said savagely, "You believe in the Bible, stranger?"

"Sure, but that's not what—"

"I'll thank ye not to mock the work of the Lord," he said. He went on swearing in the jury. Eddie did not take his hat off. He lay sprawled on his back, shoving cartridges from a box into the empty spaces in his gun belt. When the old man turned to swear him in Eddie had dumped the shells from his Colt onto his hand and he was wiping them one by one on his jeans. The old man held out the Bible. Eddie yawned, shifted the Colt to his left hand, and placed the right palm on the Bible.

The old man jerked the Bible away.

"Young whippersnapper!" he shouted. "You put away that godless piece of junk an' stand up 'n' take off your hat like a God-fearin' man, else I ain't gonna swear you in!"

"Don' wanna be swore in," muttered Eddie. "Whyn't we jus' hoist 'im now? I mean, why we foolin' around?"

"Get yourself swore in, Eddie," Sheridan said calmly. "We owe our guest a little courtesy. Now you jus' put away your toy an' stand up like a good boy an' do what yore Uncle Dave says. Hear me, boy?"

"Was wipin' the oil offa my shells," Eddie mumbled.

"Uncle Dave's been here since the year one. Only the mountains been here longer. When he tells you to do somethin', *do it*."

"Put too much oil on m' shells," Eddie mumbled in an aggrieved tone, but he did as he was told.

Uncle Dave swore Eddie in. When he had finished, Sheridan turned to Slocum and said, "Jury's swore. Want a defense lawyer? Pick anyone here. Pick me, if you want. Pick Uncle Dave, only I gotta warn you, you shot his brother. But if I tell 'im to be your lawyer, he's gonna be your lawyer."

Slocum wanted to play for time until he could use his hand again. He was standing almost exactly between Eddie's Colt and the gun belt hanging on its nail. But there would be no point at all in grabbing for a gun when he still could not hold it in his hand. He flexed his fingers as unobtrusively as possible and said, "I want this trial held in the county seat."

The expected burst of laughter came from the group.

Sheridan lay back in his hammock and kicked off again. He grinned as the hammock began its slow oscillations.

"Now," he said lazily, "that would jus' inconvenience ev'ryone mighty bad, what with roundup time jus' about here. An' if we did get enough jurors, why, they'd still be kin, or at least dependent on my good will, so you wouldn't get a fair trial. Or you'd get people with mighty unpleasant things said about them—like people sayin' they'd brand anythin' with a hide, from a tambourine to a buff'lo. An' when men like *that* sit on a jury, they lean over backwards to show how much they disapprove of other citizens goin' 'round knockin' down bobwire 'n' trespassin' 'n' shootin' ol' men. Why, Mr. Pearson, how could a man expect justice from them? An' then they'd hang you under painful circumstances, bein' without experience. So let's save time an' save the county the expense of a trial. Because these gennelmen here ain't expectin' to be paid for jury duty. They'll save the county money. You gotta keep that in mind, Mr. Pearson. So who you want for a lawyer?"

"Lookin' around here at the legal talent," Slocum said, "I'll be my own lawyer, thank you." The blood was beginning to flow back into his fingers. It felt as if sharp little needles were digging into his hands, but he could feel that control was coming back.

Sheridan grinned at Slocum's last remark. "All right, Sam," he said. "What's your evidence that Mr. Pearson here trespassed?"

"His cattle was down by the tank."

"You know how to read, mister?" Sheridan asked Slocum.

"Yep."

"You see that sign up by the tank?"

"Yep."

"You read it?"

"Yep."

"Went in anyways?"

"Yep."

"All right. Sam, what's your proof?"

"Proof? Hell, I saw the wire down!"

Sheridan turned to Slocum. "Wanna deny anythin' said here?"

"Nope."

Sheridan's eyebrows lifted slightly. He had expected more of a fight. His expression showed that clearly to Slocum. Then he shrugged. "All right, Sam. What's the evidence on the murder charge?"

Sam silently placed a dirty forefinger in the center of his forehead. "Big blue hole," he said, "smack in the middle."

"Middle?"

"Dead center."

Sheridan's eyes focused on Slocum. Now Slocum's fingers felt as if tiny little knives were being twisted around each bone, spiraling down toward each fingertip.

"Handy with a .45?"

Slocum shrugged.

"You got no record. I checked up. You ain't big enough to get your picture took. You musta run out of whiskey bottles to shoot at."

Slocum smiled secretly. His record was written all over the West, but he had left a trail of aliases, and he was able to change his appearance easily by growing a beard or cutting his hair short. It was no wonder Sheridan couldn't find anything out in three or four days. And Slocum had made very sure to keep his nose clean in this part of Arizona, where he had his little spread.

"He swung a double-barreled shotgun on me," he told Sheridan.

Sheridan looked at Sam, who said, "No shotgun."

"You're lyin' to me, boy," Sheridan said. He stared at Slocum in a blend of hard anger and suppressed amusement.

"Then what the hell blew the leg off my horse?"

"What horse?" asked Hannum, grinning. "Di'n't find no horse."

The knives were gouging away at his fingers worse than ever. Slocum set his lips against the pain; his only chance was to prolong the trial as long as possible, until he could finally get control of his hands. Now they felt as if they were being put through a meat grinder.

"How'd I get there?" he demanded of Hannum.

"Mebbe yuh rode one o' your cows," Hannum said with a nasty smile.

"Got one more charge 'gainst you, Pearson," Sheridan said. "Horse stealin'. Where'd you git the horse you were ridin' when they picked you up down in old Mexico?"

"Bought it."

"Where's the receipt?"

"Didn't ask for one."

"But you bought it?"

"Yep."

"Fair 'n' square?"

"Yep."

"Ah," Sheridan said. "Fair 'n' square, he says."

The bar of sunlight that had been striped across Sheridan's silver and ebony gun had shifted a few inches lower to his holster. The butt itself was in shadow, and the small silver inlays glowed in the dark wood like little moons. Slocum wished silently for ten more minutes of talk. That would suffice for his circulation to return enough so that he could function—he hoped. Sheridan took the cigar out of his mouth and examined the end, savoring both the cigar and the moment.

"You insist on that?" he asked Slocum.

"Yeah."

"Bring 'im in, Sam."

Sam went to the door and yelled, "You! C'mere!"

The old miner walked in. Slocum stared.

"Recognize 'im?" asked Sheridan.

"Sure!" Slocum said. "Ask him. He knows about the horse."

"This man buy your horse?" asked Sheridan.

"No," said the miner. He was pale and his eyes avoided Slocum's astonished stare.

"No—what?" prodded Sheridan, with a wide smile.

"He done stole it."

"How?"

"He stuck me up 'n' took it."

"How much he give you for the horse? Better tell the truth in this here court."

"Nothin'."

"Sure now?"

"Yep," the miner muttered. He kept staring at the floor. It was obvious to Slocum that the man had been terrorized into giving false testimony. Even in the midst of Slocum's helpless rage he managed to find some pity for the miner.

"Anythin' to say to that?" asked Sheridan, turning toward Slocum.

"Yep." Slocum's cold, casual tone brought Sheridan's heavy head upwards. He stared at Slocum with renewed interest. Someone had dumped Slocum's saddlebags beside the hammock. Sheridan reached down, picked them up, and idly unbuckled and rebuckled them. Slocum's apparent lack of fight was beginning to bore Sheridan.

"Well?" he asked, not even looking at Slocum any more.

"I could take a witness like that," Slocum said slowly, "and prove that Jesus Christ ran a whorehouse on Cienaga Creek. You bet. A whorehouse on the Cienaga."

Sheridan came alive again. He slapped his thigh with delight. He turned to the old miner, who had flushed red.

"Whatddya say to that?" Sheridan demanded. "You been accused of perjury, man!"

The miner swallowed nervously. He mumbled, "I done tolc you, Mr. Sheridan. He stole my horse. An' my saddle. An' my Winchester."

"My, my! Let's add it all up. Trespassin'. Destruction of property. Murder. Horse stealin'."

"That's only four," Slocum said. "How about larceny for the saddle and the Winchester? That'll make it a full house."

His fingers were almost back to normal, he thought.

Sheridan chuckled. He looked almost affectionately at Slocum. Then he turned to the jury. None of them shared his amusement.

"Well, gennelmen," he said genially, "time for the verdict. Anyone see any reason why he ain't guilty?"

After a few seconds of silence Sheridan turned back to Slocum. "Reckon we'll have to hang you. That's democracy, friend. You wanna write a letter to anyone, I'll see they get it."

"Got no one."

"Sure now? It won't be no trouble," Sheridan said. Slocum shook his head.

"All right, Sam," Sheridan said. It was now or never.

When Sam Hannum was close enough, Slocum sank his left fist deep into Hannum's belly. It went in up to the wrist. With his right hand he reached out for the ebony-handled Colt in its holster. But his fingers had betrayed him. They refused to curl firmly around the butt. Nor could his right thumb pull back the hammer. Before he could bring his left thumb across to fan the hammer, his right hand was struck violently by his own saddlebag. Sheridan had swung it expertly and accurately at Slocum's hand. The shock of the impact knocked the gun out of his hand. It fell on the floor in front of Hannum, who was kneeling down gasping in agony. Eddie kicked the gun out of Slocum's reach and smashed his own Colt barrel against the side of Slocum's head. He staggered back and came to a halt beside one of the upright beams. He clung to it for support while his head cleared. He felt like weeping in rage at his helplessness. Blood slowly trickled down his right cheek and along his jawline. Head down, he watched a few drops drip onto his torn, filthy shirt.

He was dragged outside and boosted roughly onto the wagon seat while Eddie placed a noose around his neck. Slocum became aware of details that he knew very well were unimportant but which seemed at the time to be very important: the fibers of the rope scratched his neck. He was still furious with his own hand for betraying him. He was not terrified at the prospect of death. The scratchy rope and the pain from the gun barrel that had laid his head open prevented him from thinking about it. The rope did not have a hangman's noose on it, with the traditional thirteen turns. That meant he was intended to strangle to death instead of dying quickly of a broken neck. On his second try, Eddie managed to get the other end of the rope up and down from where the two wagon tongues were joined. He pulled in the slack, whistling tunelessly. He was grinning; this revealed his protruding canine teeth. Two of the Mexican vaqueros who worked for Sheridan took off their sombreros and crossed themselves. Slocum was still so groggy from the blow on his head that two men hopped up beside Eddie to hold him upright.

Slocum felt no fear. What he felt was rage at being so helpless, and shame for not being able to stand up like a man at the end of his life.

"All set, boys?" asked Sheridan.

Eddie placed the flat of his palm in the middle of Slocum's back, ready to push him off the seat and into the air. He nodded happily.

Sheridan walked closer. Slocum watched the slow, measured steps. He wanted the man to get real close. He had something planned for him.

"Anythin' to say?" Sheridan asked.

Slocum looked down at him from the wagon seat. His right eye was swelling rapidly.

"Y' don't look so pretty yourself right now," Eddie said.

Slocum ignored him.

"Gonna beg, boy?" Sheridan asked. He was grinning.

Slocum looked down into Sheridan's uplifted, hard, contemptuous face, and spit right into it. Then he looked up into the cottonwood tree overhead. It was full of fine white cotton from the seed pods, and as he looked, a sudden puff of wind sent thousands of tiny white flecks drifting among the green branches. Beyond the tree he could see a few old horses grazing out their last years on the rich green grass, swishing their tails to keep the deer flies off. Beyond the horses rose the blue mountains. He was sure it was going to be his last look at the world, and he wanted a good one.

Sheridan slowly wiped the saliva from his face. He was still grinning. This time he seemed pleased.

"Cut 'im down," he said.

6

"But—" Eddie began, reddening.

"I said, cut 'im down," Sheridan said gently. "Don' make me say it a third time. Then give 'im some o' your clean duds, show 'im where t' wash up, loan 'im a razor, and scrabble 'round 'n' find 'im a pair o' boots. Then I wanna see 'im."

"But the jury found 'im guilty!"

"New evidence jus' come in," Sheridan said. "I declare a mistrial." He went back inside to his hammock, sank into it, and lit another cigar. "All right, boys. Back to work," he said, calmly ignoring their angry, vicious stares. Through the blue smoke of the cigar he stared thoughtfully at his cattle grazing across the valley. From time to time, a tiny, amused smile settled on the corners of his mouth.

Slocum rubbed his hand along his smoothly shaven face. He had not shaved for three weeks. One of the Mexican vaqueros had shaved him, since he still could not hold anything firmly in his right hand. Rodolfo was very careful and had not cut him. A neat piece of adhesive covered the gash where Eddie had clubbed him. His feet were scrubbed clean, and the blisters and cuts had been smeared with an ointment that made them feel immeasurably better. He had eaten a fine meal of beef and beans and rice and tortillas. He was sitting in a deep, comfortable armchair under the cottonwood tree as dusk fell slowly from the mountains. Sheridan sat beside him in another armchair, watching the old horses munch grass.

"I pension off my old ponies an' let 'em enjoy a little peace an' free grass," Sheridan said. He leaned over and poured some more bourbon into Slocum's glass.

"Where you from, Pearson?"

Slocum came from West Virginia. He had a faint Southern accent, which he could conceal quite well, but he had long ago realized that he could never acquire the harsher northern tones convincingly. In an attempt to conceal his origin, he said "Virginia."

"Fought agin' us in the War, eh?"

Slocum nodded. He rubbed his neck where the rough fibers of the rope had left a small irritation. He lifted his glass and took a long sip. It was very good bourbon.

"I bin watchin' you, boy. Let me ramble on now. I got a proposition. Don' innerupt me. I come out here when I was small enough to run under a chicken 'n' not muss my hair. We come out in a wagon. We stopped at a little spring thirty miles north. I went out in the bushes to do my duty. I was seven years old. Twenty Apaches hit the wagon. I didn't make no sound—I had that much sense. They killed my ma 'n' pa real fast. There were ten sacks o' coffee in the wagon. They poured it on the ground. They didn't know what it was 'n' I sure wasn't goin' to tell 'em. They smashed the crate with my ma's fine china 'n' silver. They took my pa's sword, the one he wore in the war with Mexico, 'n' they busted it. When they was gone I covered up my ma 'n' pa with stones so the coyotes wouldn't get 'em 'n' I thought, if this yere country belonged to them

Apaches, I was gonna take it away from 'em. An' if they wanted t' fight me fer it, so much the better.

"Well, I took some biscuits they missed. I walked three days afore I met some teamsters comin' from Santa Fe. They buried my people, an' one of 'em sort of adopted me. When I was fifteen I struck out on my own. Got a job with a small rancher near here. Said he couldn't pay but in cattle. I worked real hard fer one year. Then I wanted out. 'What's your brand gonna be, son?' he ast me, real nice. I never had thought about that. I picked GS, fer my name. He cut out four old cows 'n' three scrawny calves from a run o' range cattle, threw 'em down on the mud flats, burned my GS on 'em, 'n' said, 'Them's your wages.'

"Later I heard he was braggin' he had given me the first degree in the cow business. Then winter closed in. The pore ol' skinny bellies 'n' swaybacks died. They was fit for nothin' but dog meat, moanin' fer help. An' I said to myself, 'There is another degree, the Royal Screw degree, 'n' I will give it to him afore I die.

"I did, too. I hadda wait twenty-four years, but I gave it to him good." Sheridan poured more bourbon into his glass and said, smiling, "You met 'im."

"Met him?"

"Why," said Sheridan, lifting his glass, and sipping it slowly while he stared at Slocum, "he's the man who swore you stole his hoss."

Slocum made his face impassive. He was silent.

"Once he used t' run ten thousand head. His house— why, his wife had glasses imported from Paris. She had a grand pianner she would paw at in one o' them Paris gowns. He had a couple sons. An' now, why, if I tole him to kiss my ass in front o' the courthouse at high noon, he'd do it. I let him keep his lil' mine. I don' want him to starve t' death. It keeps 'im goin' an' it keeps 'im handy. Ev'ry once in a while I like to dust 'im off and run 'im 'round the four counties o' this part o' the Territory, to show people what George Sheridan's Royal Screw degree looks like.''

The slow, cool wind which had been sliding down the eastern slopes of the mountains and bending the tops of the grass reached the cottonwoods. The branches heaved and stirred. Clouds of fluffy white cotton broke free and drifted down. Sheridan placed a big hand over his glass to keep the stuff out of it.

''All right, Pearson. Listen hard. Here's my proposition. I like the way you handle yourself. You come up the hard way, like I done. You think fast. You keep out o' trouble when you can. When you can't, you git into trouble fast an' you get out fast. You shoot first, an' you shoot careful. An' if your luck turns sour, you don't crawl.''

He lit a cigar and turned it slowly in his hand, staring at it. ''You're more like me than any o' my kin. Sam's so dumb he can't find his ass in the dark with his two hands. Sendin' him or Eddie t' handle somethin' is like tryin' to pour melted butter on a red-hot spoon up a wildcat's ass.

''I got a ranch here with the western border runnin' sixty-three miles in a straight line. I'm the first rancher around here to use bobwire. I got so many gates between my pastures that they hadda send me half a boxcar just full o' gate hinges. I got good friends in Washin'ton. I got somethin' big goin' here. I need a good cattleman, an' he's gotta be a good man with a gun too. I need someone who ain't afraid to break the law when it gets too confinin'. But I don't want 'im lookin' fer trouble, like that damn fool Eddie. I need someone who speaks Spanish real good. I heard you talk a bit to them vaqueros o' mine. I do a lot o' business down in Mexico.

"I want you to learn how I do business. You c'n run your cattle with mine. I'll keep tally fer you. There won't be no calves missin', neither. I *know* you cain't run your spread the way you're runnin' it now—one bad winter an' the bank'll take it all back. Ain't no one gonna risk no mortgage on your li'l place. Your next payment is due in two months. How you gonna meet it?"

Slocum shrugged. "I'll meet it," he said, but he wasn't so sure that he could.

"How? Gonna stick up a train?" asked Sheridan.

Slocum smiled to himself. Sheridan had no idea how close he was to the truth. But Slocum had decided to try to make a new life for himself. He would prefer to avoid any such thing. He had been very lucky to avoid being killed, and maybe one more holdup would be the last.

"You don't have a cent in the goddamn bank," Sheridan went on remorselessly. "I checked. You spent your last dollar buyin' that piece o' wolf bait when you reached the mountains. I'll tell you, boy, if wild geese cost ten cents a dozen you couldn't buy a hummingbird's ass."

Slocum had to smile at that one.

"First time I seen you smile, boy. I think we'll get along. Now, standard wages fer a gen'ral manager for a spread this size is three-fifty a month. I'm gonna start you at five hundred."

Slocum's eyes widened.

"Then, I'm gonna give you five per cent commission on ev'ry deal you handle for me. You'll make that mortgage payment with one hand tied behind your back. In two years you'll be able to buy your spread free 'n' clear. No one c'n take it away from you then—not even me.'' Sheridan grinned. Slocum smiled, but he didn't care for that kind of joke, not after he had seen how that miner sat up and begged like a dog whenever Sheridan chose to snap his fingers. Sheridan would bear very close watching.

''In two years,'' Sheridan repeated, ''you'll be able to buy that spread of yours free 'n' clear. Two more years, you'll be able to fence it right. Then you c'n start buyin' a couple damn fine bulls an' some prize heifers. In three more years you'll be breedin' cattle a hundred and fifty pounds heavier than any other cattle round here—'cept mine.''

''Sounds fine,'' Slocum said. ''Real fine. But I got a question. If you want me so bad, why pay me all that money just to see me leave in five years when I got my ranch going nice?''

Sheridan was delighted. He slapped his thigh in pleasure.

''*Knew* you'd ask. Because I want you to git so used to them wages you won't wanna quit. With that kind o' money you could hire yourself a good man t' run your own spread. Let someone else run that poky li'l outfit of yours. Child's play! I got somethin' *big* to play with. I expect one of these days to stand up front of my fire, shake off my Colt 'n' Winchester, an' kick 'em in 'n' watch 'em burn. I want someone I c'n trust runnin' this place then. An' mebbe you'll want to stay.''

Slocum's mind raced through all the computations: the wages, the mortgage, the prize bulls, the pile in the bank to tide him through the bad winters that were bound to come, the desire to take it easy for a while and to escape the feeling of the last ten years that there was always a marshal or a sheriff looking at him to see if he looked like the portrait on a reward poster.

He felt that Sheridan was telling the truth about himself with his wish for a strong hand to take over in the future when the man who had built up this huge ranch would be getting too old to handle all the myriad problems that were bound to come up. The realization that Sam Hannum and Eddie would hate his being around in an official capacity gave added spice to the offer.

And if he didn't like it, he could just quit and walk away, with a nice sum of money in the bank. He was a little drunk, and he knew he had better think the whole thing out very carefully before he committed himself. George Sheridan watched him carefully as he set his glass down.

"Smell your way around my proposition," Sheridan said. "Mornin's time enough. Better get some sleep. You c'n bunk in the corner."

In the morning, after a huge breakfast of beans, bacon, and tortillas Slocum leaned back and said, "All right."

Sheridan said crisply, as if he had known all along that Slocum would go along with his deal, "First thing, I want you to pick up some horses down near Nacozari. On the Rio Sonora. You'll go along with my two Mexican hands. They know their way 'round down there. I'll give you five thousand in double eagles."

That meant he'd be carrying two hundred and fifty twenty-dollar gold pieces.

"They don't want paper money," Sheridan went on, "an' silver's too heavy. The horses'll be wet."

He plunged his face into a big white basin set on a stand and washed. One of the Mexican vaqueros poured water from a white enamel pitcher into the basin and then stood back to get away from the splashing.

"Wet?"

Slocum knew what "wet" meant, but he wanted a little time to think. The word had come from Texas. It meant that the horses had crossed the Rio Grande, stolen from Mexico. If Slocum took the job and got caught, there would go his ranch. He would be back once more to square one. And if they caught him, someone would be bound to check to see if there was a reward out for him—and there were many. He could wind up serving more than thirty years.

"If you wanna back out, just say so." Sheridan wiped his face on a rough towel that one of the vaqueros handed to him. He looked out at his meadows as the cloud shadows raced over them. The faint contempt in his voice stung like acid. "You're gonna earn your money workin' fer me, Pearson. Yes or no?"

"Yes," Slocum said. It would be safer than sticking up a bank, anyway.

7

Sheridan rode with Slocum and the two Mexicans as far as the gate. The Mexicans took off their sombreros and he shook hands with them formally. Then he shook hands with Slocum. It was the first time they had ever touched, and Slocum felt for the first time how hard the man's hand was. He could feel Sheridan's gold ring cutting into his knuckle as the man sat looking at his face with a half quizzical, half intrigued smile. Then he said, "Good luck!" and he turned and rode back.

The Mexicans put on their dusty sombreros. Tito and his companion, Rodolfo, showed no inclination to talk to Slocum. This seemed a bit odd, and as they rode a little behind, showing him the deference expected from inferiors, something seemed wrong to Slocum. He couldn't put his finger on it, but perhaps, he decided, it was because they were too quiet. They rolled *cigarillos* of the pungent, strong Mexican tobacco and talked softly in Spanish. Once Tito pulled his carbine from its scabbard as his horse shied at a coiled rattler that refused to give way. The first shot blew its head away.

"After God, my Winchester," he said, grinning as he ejected the used shell. He pulled a fresh one from his bandolier and inserted it as the horse edged nervously from the writhing coils.

Each of Slocum's saddlebags held 125 gold double eagles. The Mexicans earned twenty dollars a month.

Slocum felt sure they were completely loyal to Sheridan. Why would he send them if he did not trust them? But two Mexicans would behave very differently in Mexico than they would in Arizona, he felt sure. He decided to keep a narrow watch, but not in such a way that they would notice and take offense. Mexican pride was a touchy affair, and he would have to walk carefully.

The money would be a temptation for him, too. As they rode south he let his mind linger over the gold coins. It could buy him a very nice little spread down in Mexico. Sheridan was no fool, and he would have considered that as well. Slocum decided at last that Sheridan expected all three of them to keep careful watch on one another. He grinned to himself, admiring the man. He felt fine. His hand could hold a gun again. Eddie's spare clothes fit him decently enough, although they were a bit tight. He was pleased that his first month's salary would let him meet the next mortgage payment on his spread. The hot sun forced the pungent aroma out of the sage. He was lulled by the comfortable creak of the saddle leather under him. He began to whistle.

Slocum had underestimated Sheridan. The man was hard and complex. He had built himself a small kingdom with his toughness and shrewdness.

There was no one in that part of the territory who dared challenge him. Victory was his, but the taste of it had gone flat in his mouth. For a couple of years he used to swing in his hammock with his spurs gouging out the grooves Slocum had noticed in the same plank, smoking cigars and thinking. He slept badly. George Sheridan could not put his finger on what troubled him. Part of it, he knew, was the loss of his son, to whom he had planned to leave his kingdom. The rest of it he had not been able to decipher.

And one day he suddenly realized what the trouble was. What had been exhilarating all through the early years was not merely the acquisition of cattle and the rangeland which kept circling his small first ranch like the growth rings on a sequoia. Nor was it the deference shown him whenever he went to Austin or Omaha or Chicago.

What he really loved, he finally realized, was the struggle itself: the fight with the savage, hard-bitten men who wanted the two things he wanted himself—land and power.

In the beginning it was the occasional Apache war party that made every night suspenseful. When he had built his fortress on the Madrona, and when he had hired plenty of good men, the cemetery on the ridge began to fill up with Apache graves as well as others. After that, the war parties began to avoid his ranch. It was too costly for their scant manpower. For the last two years, not a single attack had been made on the old retired cowpuncher who plowed the rich river bottom acres for potatoes and onions with a carbine scabbard strapped to the plow handle.

It took some time before Sheridan realized that he actually missed the war parties, missed the occasional defiant yell from the ridge opposite and the scalp waved from the top of a long lance.

Then, when the ranch began to grow seriously, his new enemies appeared. These were the ranchers whose land and water he coveted. If they were poor, they fought him themselves with their sons. If they were rich, they hired professional gunfighters. Sheridan enlisted his kin from back East, as well as a few professionals, and for fifteen years the bitter war went on. A second cousin of his would be blasted from ambush with a shotgun. Perhaps he in turn would catch a man branding one of his calves with a running iron.

Savagely maintaining that the calf had been stolen from his own herd—and frequently telling the truth, as Sheridan well knew—the man would be hanged in five minutes from a piñon branch if he had been caught in the mountains, or from a saguaro in the dry country.

Without opposition, the even, uneventful flow of days bored him. His life had lost its salt.

When he was watching Slocum stand on the wagon seat with Eddie's palm in the middle of his back, ready to send him into eternity, Sheridan suddenly realized that up there was the man for whom he had been searching for years without knowing it—a man who could give him a glorious fight.

Slocum, Sheridan had noticed, was tough and intelligent. He was a fast thinker—and a man with a ranch no bigger than Sheridan's when he himself had first settled there, because the Apaches wouldn't like it. Slocum's little ranch was a nucleus, and it could grow, but only at the expense of the ranches surrounding it. And Sheridan owned or controlled all the ranch property and all the water rights surrounding Slocum's place.

If Slocum could be nursed along with money, Sheridan mused, with a taste of power, and with a knowledge of how to use both—if he could learn how to handle local and state law enforcement officers—if he were to be introduced to the right people with whom to deal up in Flagstaff—why, then the man might break away and go all out against him.

But only a rich and powerful man would put up a fight worth any interest.

Therefore, Sheridan would make it his job to see that Slocum became rich and powerful. Slocum must never find out that he was being gentled along for this purpose. A man like Slocum, Sheridan felt instinctively, would never stand being handled as if he were a toy, even if he were to become rich by it. He had to feel that all the decisions were his and his alone. And he must never find out why George Sheridan wanted him so badly.

But since Pearson was designated for such a high destiny, Sheridan brooded as he swung to and fro in his hammock, he would first have to pass a few severe tests. He'd have to be tested in the field, as it were. And Sheridan devoutly hoped that Slocum would pass with flying colors.

The first test was simple: he had ordered the two Mexican vaqueros to kill Slocum as soon as they crossed the border into Sonora.

8

Slocum suddenly woke to the sound of a sharp *click!*

Across the small campfire he could see that Tito had just pumped a cartridge into the chamber of his Winchester. He had done it under his blanket to muffle the sound. Now Slocum watched him pull it out and raise it.

The other man placed a hand on his arm and whispered in Spanish, "Let him have a good rest; pretty soon he'll begin his trip to the other world." Tito shrugged, nodded, and lowered the carbine until it rested across his knees.

Slocum was a little surprised, but not much. He trusted no one where money was involved—especially plenty of it. His head lay on his saddle slicker. Underneath the slicker was his Colt in its holster. Luckily, he was lying on his stomach. Slowly his hand inched up under the blanket as the two men idly smoked their cigarillos, allowing him a few more minutes of life before the bullet would smash into his skull. The Winchester was pointed directly at him. All that was needed was the slightest pull on the trigger. Any suspicion on Tito's part that Slocum was awake would be sufficient for Tito to shoot.

Then Slocum heard a dry whirring noise, like the sound of a rattler warning someone not to come any closer. Slocum realized that Rodolfo was spinning his

.45 cylinder with his left hand. So he was ready too. They were looking at him, Slocum was sure of that. They were probably mildly regretting what they were about to do. There was nothing personal in it. That was the Mexican philosophy. Death came to all men sooner or later, and a little shove was not so terrible.

Most likely, Slocum thought, the .45 in Rodolfo's hand was pointing at him as a backup for Tito. Infinitely slowly, Slocum's hand curled around the butt of his Colt.

He threw the blanket aside and came up shooting.

Tito half rose, took one stumbling step, and fell choking into the campfire. Reflex action made him pull the trigger. The bullet seared Slocum's neck. His second shot broke Rodolfo's right shoulder and knocked him backward off the flat stone on which he was sitting. His right arm was useless. He scrambled frantically for the Colt in the darkness with his left hand. Slocum was standing now. He saw the Colt and kicked it out of range.

"Hijo de la chingada!" said Rodolfo, still on his knees. His right arm dangled as he made the sign of the cross with his left hand. He bowed his head and waited. If Rodolfo had not asked Tito to give Slocum a little more time, Slocum knew that he himself would have died. But if he were to let Rodolfo live, the man would become an implacable enemy for the rest of his life. Slocum looked down at Rodolfo, still kneeling. His head was bowed as if he were in front of an altar. Then he fired.

"Where's them two Mex'cans?" asked Pete Watts. He leaned back in his office chair and let the gold coins slip through his fingers as if they were poker chips.

Slocum looked through the dirty plate-glass window at the sunken street of Nacozari. The elaborately curlicued gold scroll letters on the glass read P. WATTS RANCH PROPETIES.

"Goddam Mex'can sign painter can't spell decent," Watts grunted. " 'n' don't tell me it's because he don't know English. The son of a bitch murders the Spanish signs too."

Watts dealt in ranches south of the border. He pieced off every official in the state of Sonora, including any general stationed in the vicinity. As a result he was graciously permitted to continue functioning, on the simple theory that if one has a honey bee which produces honey when pressed, one should let him gather honey. And that was something this bee did better than any Mexican real-estate operator in Sonora.

"Look at *that!*" he suddenly said indignantly. He pointed across the street to a sign heralding a pulqueria. It read PULQERIA. "See? See what I mean?" he demanded. "Where's the Mex'cans? I ast you oncet."

"We got into an argument," Slocum said. Watts looked at the hard, thin face with the tight lips. The green eyes stared at him with an unnerving, level stare. Watts decided to drop the subject.

"Damn shame," he growled. "They was good men. How you gonna take seventy-three pieces of wolf bait up to George Sheridan's place all by yourself, I dunno. Why'n'cha try to get 'em back? I got no men to spare."

"When I take delivery of the horses, I'll start worryin'. Right now it's no never mind. Gimme a bill of sale."

"I don't give no bills of sale."

Slocum pushed the stacks of double eagles into his saddlebags and started for the door.

Watts stood up. His pale, square face had reddened.

"People 'round here don't behave like that to me—" he began, but Slocum cut him off abruptly.

"Bill of sale or not?"

"Look here, Pearson. That's your name, ain't it?" he asked, with a cynical little smile. He looked at the cold face and suddenly realized he was skating on very thin ice. It was bad manners to make any sort of reference to a man's current name. People had died for this breach of etiquette, and Watts was shrewd enough to know that here was someone who would kill him without compunction if necessary.

"Look here," he started again, with an effort at friendliness, "didn't George explain things?"

"What do you mean?"

"People come down into Mexico lookin' for stolen horses. I deal in horses. I ain't too perticular sometimes as to whose horses I deal in. Plenty of horses we get down here got brands registered north of the border. Sometimes as far north as Wyoming, by God."

"Suppose someone starts to ask questions when I go north with the horses?"

Watts grinned. "Why," he said softly, "that's where a couple of good men like Rodolfo and Tito come in handy, see?"

Slocum looked without expression at Watts. Watts felt uneasy. If the man opposite him, he thought, would only show some sort of reaction, then he, Watts, would know how to react in turn. But not having the faintest idea what Slocum was thinking made him nervous.

Watts said reassuringly, "Just say you bought 'em offen me. I'll back you up."

Slocum's eyebrows rose slightly. Again there was no other expression. Watts waited tensely. Watts was a tough man, used to dealing with rustlers and horse thieves and the varied groups of *bandidos* who were out for anything they could grab—and the revolutionaries, who announced that they would have to take a man's life, or gun, or horse, or woman, for a better Mexico.

"No offense meant," Slocum said, "but if they're gonna come to you to find out if I bought 'em from you, and you say you're gonna back me up, why not give me the bill of sale right away? That backs me, and no time wasted telegraphin' you to check on my story. Or my neck getting stretched by an overanxious deputy."

"Between here an' George's ranch you ain't gonna meet no overanxious deputy. No one 'round here or up in Arizona is gonna risk stirrin' up that man. Would you stick your hand in a sow grizzly's mouth?"

"*Adiós*," Slocum said. He couldn't get satisfaction from Watts, so he would see what he could do by himself.

He stepped out into the brilliant glare of noon. The saddlebags were slung over his shoulder. The town of Nacozari, beaten flat by the white-hot quiver of the sun, panted, crouching like a dog, waiting until late afternoon, when it would rise to shake off the pitiless blanket of heat.

Nacozari existed because it lay on the old Spanish road to the Navajo and Apache country. Wagonmasters had laid it out centuries ago. It was a good road for the transport of cattle to the Apache reservation, where Indian agents bought them.

Before Slocum could put his foot into the stirrup Watts was calling him back. When Watts had finished writing out the bill of sale, Slocum upended the saddle-bags over the desk once more. He asked Watts to recommend two good men to help him drive the horses north.

Within ten minutes Watts had produced a tall, thin redhead named Jenkins, who wore steel spurs set close to his heels with a solid rowel three inches across. On a horse's flank it would have the effect of a circular saw. Noticing Slocum's critical glance, Jenkins said, "Sure makes 'em get a wiggle on theirselves, don't it?"

"You bet," Slocum said. He rejected the man. Next he rejected two men Watts produced out of a dark room in the back where they had been sleeping. "God damn it, Pearson," Watts said, sounding annoyed, "I don't know what the hell you're lookin' for, I really don't!"

"Thank you kindly for your help," Slocum said, unmoved. He went to the nearest livery stable and had his horse fed and curried. He asked a small boy working in the stable if he knew any vaqueros who wanted work. He said that his two uncles were vaqueros, they lived in San Ildefonso de Temosachic, pretty close, and would the señor wait till the evening, when they would come, of a certainty?

Slocum waited, and the two vaqueros came. They were in their late forties and had the shriveled mahogany skin and calloused hands of old cowpunchers. Their spurs had small rowels, and their horses looked in good health. When they pulled the saddles off and squatted for a talk with him, Slocum noticed that their horses' backs did not have any sores. From the center of each cinch, under the horses' bellies, hung a red, braided tassel of dyed horsehair. The men looked good to Slocum, and they said they would come with him.

9

"Watts give you any trouble?"

Slocum shrugged.

"What he say 'bout the Mexicans?"

"Nothin'. Just told him I'd gotten rid of 'em."

George Sheridan grunted. He came out of the hammock with the swift ease that always surprised Slocum.

"Watts don't like me, Pearson. Which means he don't like you neither. You bury them two?"

Slocum shook his head.

"Plenty *zapilotes* around?" *Zapilotes* were regarded as the official garbage disposal unit of Mexico.

"Yeah."

"*Zapilotes* might make people go out fer a looksee," Sheridan said, stretching his big heavy arms and shoulders. "An' if they find anythin' Watts'll hear 'bout it."

"He never struck me as a man who cared what happened to a couple of Mexicans."

"Yeah, that's true. But he don't like me, an' you wind up some day down around his territory he'll let them know. Ever been in a Mex jail?"

Slocum had been in a few in his time, but he denied it.

"They don' feed you. Your relatives feed you. You don't got relatives, you don' eat. But you ain't gonna be there long enough to get hungry, 'cause

60

you'll be shot tryin' to escape. Even if you *ain't* tryin' to escape.''

"*Ley fuga?*"

"*Ley fuga*, you bet. Law of escape.'' Sheridan lit a cigar. "God damn it,'' he said, without anger or passion, "an' I had somethin' lined up fer you to do down there.''

He looked hard at Slocum. "It's risky,'' he went on. "Trouble is, got no one else who's got the sand or the brains fer it.''

"I'm takin' your money,'' Slocum said calmly.

"I ain't pushin' you, Pearson. Think it over.''

"I thought it over.''

"You shoot them Mexicans this side of the river, or down in Mexico?''

"Mexico.''

"Um,'' Sheridan said. "I want to show you somethin'.''

They walked across the hard-packed yard. Scattered along the walls of the adobe house were traces of the flower beds Sheridan's wife had started, and which he had let go to seed after her death.

He stopped in front of a low, strongly built adobe shed.

"Watts'll soon find out that them Mexicans ain't been seen 'round any of those little towns in Sonora. That'll give the son of a bitch somethin' to chew on. He likes to sit in that little office of his an' chew. He figgers sooner or later you'll be back Nacozari way. Then he'll take that cud of his he's been chewin' an' look at it again. He's got good friends 'round there, they tell 'im things. I'm tellin' you, boy, you are gonna put your paw into a bear trap.'' He took a big key from his pocket and fitted it into a huge padlock. "You sure you wanna go ahead?"

"I don't like Mr. Watts. I got an itch to see if he can close that trap fast enough to catch my paw."

Sheridan chuckled. Slocum thought he didn't seem too disturbed for a man who had just lost two good vaqueros. "Y' say the click of the carbine lever is what woke yuh?"

"Yeah."

"Sleep real light?"

"Lately I do."

"Yes," Sheridan said, "we must remember that."

He unlocked the door. The room was filled with wooden crates. Some were long, some were square. The long ones were marked SHOVELS. The square ones were parked CHISELS.

Sheridan kicked one of the long cases. "Winchesters," he grunted. He kicked a square box and looked inquiringly at Slocum.

"Somethin' tells me they aren't chisels."

"Y' win a cigar," Sheridan said, with a broad grin. "Cartridges."

He locked up. When they were outside he went on. "I ain't fixin' to start no war. But someone else is. An' he's gonna pay plenty for those. In the shape of cattle. You're gonna meet 'im in Mexico."

"Down in Sonora?"

"Yep. Wanna back out?"

"I haven't said so."

"If y' get into trouble y' better hit the border at a dead run, Pearson. They play rough down there. I'm sendin' Sam with you. That sheriff's star might carry some weight. Professional courtesy. Now come on back and I'll tell you what to do. An' you better pray they don' find out about you an' them two Mexicans.

That afternoon the wagon was loaded. The boxes of cartridges covered the bottom of the big freighter. On top were the crates marked SHOVELS. On top of those rolls of barbed wire were thrown. Sheridan gave Slocum a sheet of paper.

It was a written order from Watts, on his stationery. It ordered a hundred and fifty shovels, to be crated in boxes of ten each, sixty boxes of chisels, and fifty rolls of barbed wire. The order was written in Sheridan's handwriting. The ink was still wet. Sheridan had come out of the house waving the paper in the air. Slocum grinned while he folded the paper carefully and put it inside his wallet.

"Watts is a much nicer pusson than you think," Sheridan said. "He gimme lots of these. The bobwire is to discourage casual look-sees. See if you c'n sell the stuff to Watts."

"Sure," Slocum said. "After all, he ordered the stuff."

Sheridan slapped his thigh. "By God, he did, di'n't he?" He laughed uproariously.

Sam Hannum sat silently on the corral fence and watched Sheridan count out a thousand dollars in double eagles.

"Expense money," the big man said. While Slocum packed the gold pieces into his saddlebags, Sheridan lowered his voice. "I bin watchin' Sam," he said. "Funny as hell to watch that slab-sided face of his thinkin' away there. I c'n practic'ly hear the gears workin'. He jus' can't figger you. He's been like that ever since he heard how yuh shot Rodolfo 'n' Tito. He's a little smarter'n most of my kin. Which ain't sayin' much. Reminds me of that Mex sayin'—you know the one?—'In the country of the blind, the one-eyed man is king.' "

Sheridan grinned. "Well, the others been sayin' you kilt them two vaqueros of mine in cold blood. I don't hold with that. They're fixin' to get you."

"Why the hell should I shoot two men in cold blood? They didn't have money; they didn't have a goddamn thing I wanted."

"Everybody knows that. But you mighta shot 'em because they was loyal to me. Until the night you caught one of 'em workin' the lever of his Winchester. If that's what happened."

"That's what happened."

"Yeah," said Sheridan. The tone made Slocum turn around and look at him. Sheridan was smiling at him. "That's what happened. I tol' that to the boys. But they wanted to cut you down. None of 'em believe you're loyal to me, jus' 'cause I saved you from bein' hanged. Who put the rope 'round your neck? Ol' George Sheridan! So why wouldn't you reconsider the whole business, deep in Mexico with all that gold to reconsider with? Why not? That's what they said. Heard 'em. So whaddya do? Shot 'em in their sleep. Tol' 'em you'd take the next guard an' then shot 'em when you heard 'em snorin' away. Ol' Tito, now, he really could snore. Now, Pearson, I ask yuh, what's wrong with that thinkin'?"

"Then why did I come back?"

Sheridan lifted one finger like an old-fashioned preacher about to admonish a sheepish congregation. "Who knows what lies in the heart of a man?" he said, in sonorous tones. "Mebbe you figgered no one'd ever think you kilt 'em if you came back. Mebbe you didn't want to live down in Mexico; mebbe you don't like *frijoles*. I sure as hell don't know. I done tole 'em you did right. But you better watch 'em all."

"I hear Eddie's a good shot."

"None better. Best I ever seen with a carbine. He might have pimples, but I seen 'im shoot the lock off the post office door at a full gallop. He wasn't fixin' to rob it, he jus' took on a bet he could do it. I hadda write a letter to the federal marshal an' to Washin'ton to make 'em fergit it. Damn fool. He can't make no distinction between a fed'ral offense an' somethin' like a territorial land office. They wouldn't kick up hardly no fuss at all."

"I want him with me."

Sheridan was startled. "Thought you didn't like Cousin Eddie."

"Don't. But I want a good shot along."

"Gotta watch 'im. He's snotty an' he'll try to provoke you. An' he's fast."

"In Mexico, I sort of figger on him snugglin' up to me for company."

Sheridan grinned at the mental picture. "Yep," he said finally. "He'll go. He ain't gonna like it. But he'll go.

When you fixin' on leavin'?"

"Daybreak. Wanna get some things in town first."

"All right. Watch your step."

Slocum nodded and swung into his saddle. As he trotted out, Sam Hannum looked at his back. Sheridan looked also. He thought that Pearson was working out very well—very well, indeed.

10

Slocum opened his eyes and ran his hand through his newly clipped hair. It was his first haircut in months. The barber had smeared some oily pink grease over his hair just before he combed it. It looked like pink sugar frosting and smelled like the usual Mexican whorehouse, but Slocum had a fondness for it.

He felt fine. He had just made a payment on his mortgage; he was wearing a new flannel shirt and working jeans; the first sombrero he had bought in three years hung from the curved wooden hook on the opposite wall. Underneath the hat hung his gun belt, weighed down by the heavy Colt. The leather of the belt was old and cracked. He had been in too many rainstorms and had swum too many rivers; and he had neglected to rub it with saddle soap too many times. He decided to get a new one.

Steps banged into the barber shop, neared his chair, and stopped. "Gawd, he smells pretty!" Eddie said.

Slocum kept his eyes closed. "My gun's on the hook back of you," he said lazily. "Perfectly safe for you to shoot."

Eddie's voice was strangled with rage. "Think you're the king bee 'round here, don't'cha?"

Slocum still did not open his eyes. "You wanna talk to me, kid? I don't want to talk to you. Why don't you take your big bad popgun and shoot at tin cans on fence posts and pretend they're Apaches?'' He clasped his hands in front of him.

Someone outside the shop yelled, ''He's callin' you, Eddie! Gonna put somethin' in the kitty or yuh gonna let 'im take the pot?'' The barber slid the mirror to one side.

Slocum opened his eyes and said quietly, ''Leave that mirror there, mister. I wanna see what you did.'' As Slocum thought, Eddie had obviously been mentioning his plans to the whole town. It seemed to Slocum that everyone in town was standing on the board sidewalk, staring through the filthy window. A potted fern which had died years ago hung from the ceiling in front of the window. A few men had ducked low in order to peer underneath it.

Sam Hannum was nowhere in sight. Slocum decided that this was because if he were around he'd have to make an attempt to keep the peace. Slocum closed his eyes once more.

''Well, Eddie,'' said the disappointed barber, ''look at 'im. He ain't even gonna open his eyes while you talk. That's downright disrespectable.''

'' 'Insolent' is the word you're lookin' for, barber. And the word for you is 'stupid.' ''

Eddie grabbed the dirty white sheet the barber had draped over Slocum. He jerked it to the floor. Slocum kept his eyes closed and his face impassive.

''That 'nough, for you, yella belly?'' Eddie shouted. His hand hovered over his gun butt.

Slocum opened his eyes lazily. He completely ignored the shouting youth. He behaved as if Eddie were not there. He looked in the mirror and motioned to the barber to hold a small mirror behind him. He critically examined the back of his neck and passed his hand over it.

"Not too—" he began.

"I ain't gonna shoot you in the back, goddamn it! Turn around!"

"—bad at all," Slocum finished amiably. He grinned at Eddie's furious reflection. He knew nothing serious would happen in front of a crowd as long as he was unarmed. If he had been wearing his gun he was not sure what the stupid boy might do.

"I'm not turnin' around," he remarked to Eddie's reflection.

"What I gotta do to make you draw?" Eddie asked, almost plaintively.

"Why," Slocum said, as if he were humoring a bad-tempered child, "I'll put on my gun. Maybe I'll give you all the excitement you want, an' maybe not. Depends on how I feel. You treat me right, maybe I'll put it on. You talk bad to me, maybe I won't put it on. Maybe I'll just walk out of here backwards. You just gotta be patient till I make up my mind."

A few men guffawed.

Eddie was no fool. He knew the longer Slocum stretched out the situation, the more ridiculous he would look. He spun around, grabbed Slocum's gun belt, and tossed it to Slocum.

"Get goin'!" he said.

Slocum held the belt in his left hand. He unbuckled it very slowly. Eddie trembled with impatience.

"You better sit down, Mr. Edward," Slocum observed kindly. The tone infuriated Eddie. Slocum stopped his unbuckling and peered at Eddie, full of solicitude.

"Indeed, you better," Slocum went on. "You're gonna die of a stroke if you don't. The chair I'm sittin' in is mighty comfortable. Please take it. I don't mind standin' while I try to fix this here buckle."

He got out of the chair and politely stood aside for Eddie.

"Come on, come *on!*" Eddie said. His voice was almost out of control by now. "You got that damn buckle open!"

"Ain't," Slocum said.

More snickers came from the men outside. They acted like sandpaper upon Eddie's sensitive mood.

"Git it open, goddamn it!"

"I wanna live a little longer," said Slocum in a plaintive manner. Everyone outside was grinning by now.

He slowly spread the belt open. Eddie watched every movement with almost unbearable intensity, clenching and unclenching his gun hand. Slocum opened the belt wide. He stopped and poised his hands in the air, far apart.

"Sure you don't wanna rest in the chair while you wait?" he asked solicitously, indicating the chair he had just vacated.

A loud chuckle burst from the crowd. Eddie spun and glared at them. Then he turned back to face Slocum. Slocum very slowly buckled on his belt. He lifted his hands and poised them. Eddie was tense and white-faced.

"Wanna ask a question," Slocum said amiably.

Eddie almost wept in vexation.

"Question is," Slocum asked, with a serious expression, "if I put my hands down to pull my belt one notch tighter, like, will you get excited?"

"Pull it tighter! Jesus Christ!"

Very slowly Slocum lowered his hands. He pulled the belt tighter.

"Reason why I want the belt tighter," he began conversationally, "is because—"

"I don't give a goddamn why you want it tighter," Eddie shouted. "Just draw!"

Slocum took his hands off the buckle. He placed both hands at shoulder level. Then he opened and closed them a few times while he looked at Eddie.

"You ready—" Eddie began.

But, as the barber said later to George Sheridan, describing what happened, "I never seed nothin' so fast. *Never*. Eddie had just about pulled the bottom of the barrel of his Colt offen the bottom of his holster by the time Pearson had jammed his Colt about three inches deep into Eddie's left ear. Eddie, he just stood there, all froze up, his mouth open like he was laid out in the back of Scanlan's Funeral Parlor. He was so surprised he wasn't even scairt. Then he thought fer a while, an' *then* he got scairt, so scairt he couldn't even swaller. *I* swallered. I was scairt it was the end o' Eddie, an' him owin' me fer five haircuts."

"What happened next?" Sheridan grunted.

"Pearson whispers somethin' into Eddie's ear. I was the only one who heard 'im; I was close. He said, 'You c'n push a gun till you're dead, sonny.' Then he pulled Eddie's Colt. Then he picked up the shavin' brush an' he looked at the wet lather in the bowl. I swear fer a minute I thought he was gonna smear it over Eddie's face, teach him a lesson. Then he looked at Eddie's face, an' smiled, an' put the brush back. Then he shook the bullets outa Eddie's Colt an' put it back in the holster. 'Take your hands down,' he said. 'An' do me a favor. Don't give your gun to anyone when I'm gone.'

"Well, I thought the whole damn crowd would go into convulsions. Eddie bust out like a ball out of a chute. He picked up his hoss on those big Mex spurs he just bought, an' when he set 'im down he was runnin' at his best, an' you could hear rocks fallin' for ten minutes." He chuckled.

Sheridan said slowly, "Eddie's sure lucky. He better cool off, the crazy son of a bitch. All he's got on his mind is to prove how tough he is. Pearson don't have to prove that to anyone. If Eddie pushes 'im once more I'm afraid it's gonna be another case of slow. But I got somethin' for 'im to do. Hope it keeps 'im outa trouble. An' he might grow up—which he better do fast, before he stops livin' completely."

It took the slow wagon two weeks to reach Nacozari. Eddie was his usual sullen self. He had a filthy poker deck and in the evenings he played solitaire until he was sleepy. Sam Hannum, on the other hand, would ride ahead of the wagon. If Slocum should chance to ride ahead, then Hannum would silently drop to the rear.

One morning they found one of the horses gone and a worn-out Apache moccasin left in its place. Slocum knew immediately it was a very clear message from the Apache who had stolen it—a Chiricahua, by the design of the moccasin—that he was tired of walking.

"We comin' back this way?" Eddie demanded. Slocum said yes; it was the shortest way. Eddie said they'd have trouble for sure. He played no more solitaire in the evenings, but sat, tense, with his carbine on his lap.

When Slocum finally walked into the office, Watts was sitting behind his desk doodling on his blotter.

Before Slocum could get out a word Watts held up his hand.

"Bring the shovels 'n' chisels?" he asked.

"Yeah."

"Who you got to watch the stuff?"

Slocum jerked his thumb. Watts got up and walked to the window. He sat down again heavily and said, "Jesus. *Those* two."

Slocum almost felt a surge of friendliness for him.

"Well," Watts sighed, "if that's what you got, that's what you got. Sheridan tell you what you're s'pposed to do now?"

"Yeah. Saragoza."

"What else he say?"

"That's all."

"That ain't so good. Saragoza is where them two Mex come from—the ones you *fired*." Watts emphasized the last word very slightly as he spoke. "It's been noticed in Saragoza that they ain't been back since they went through here with you. An' they ain't written to their mamas, neither. I'd say right now it wouldn't be too healthy for you to set foot anywhere in Mexico for a while. Best thing is for you to go back." He smiled. "So I better handle the deal myself."

"Pretty dangerous 'round here, then?"

"For you, yes. For me, no. I got plenty of friends down here, Pearson."

"You get along?"

"I get along, yes."

"You're supposed to introduce me to the man in Saragoza, that right?"

"That's right," Watts said lazily.

"And the way things are, you figger I better stay here while you go over and fix everythin', right?"

"Right. It'll be safer—"

"Yeah. I know, Watts. And you'll take those shovels and chisels along?"

"Nope. I ain't that dumb. That stays in Texas."

"What the hell do you mean, *Texas?*"

Watts grinned. "Our customer is a son of a bitch. But he thinks ahead, and one thing he don't want is to get Uncle Sam pissed off at him. He thinks one day he might git to be *el presidente*. Honest. So you're gonna take that wagon, run it north again up to Benson, put it on a flatcar, run it down into Texas, take the wagon off at El Rosario, and just sit on the Rio Grande until we settle everythin'. Then we go 'n' meet on an island in the middle of the river. We start tradin'—so many cattle, so many Winchesters. Say he brings twenty head across to Texas. You bring three carbines into Mexico. If they suddenly decide to double-cross us, not too much harm done. See?"

"Why did you have us come all the goddamn way down here if we're gonna go all the way back again, for Christ's sake?"

"Because," Watts said, "he'll think he'll have us by the nuts down here in Mexico. He'll send plenty of his people here to take the wagon. But when they're comin' here, you'll be goin' east on the railroad. When he finds out you're too far for his men to grab you, he'll have to settle up fast and honest, especially since you'll be dealin' with the best hole card there is against this bastard."

"You mean I'll be in the States with the guns?"

"Right. He don't want trouble with the army or the Rangers."

"Where are the cattle?"

"Way over in Chihuahua."

"Sounds awful complicated," Slocum said.

"Yep," Watts said, almost cheerfully, "but he's a complicated man."

"Suppose you decide to double-cross him?"

"That ain't done 'round here, Pearson. People get dead. Too many little arroyos to git dry-gulched in."

Slocum permitted a look of apprehension to sweep across his face. Watts noticed it. Slocum, as soon as he knew that Watts had caught his worried expression, followed that with a look of relief. "Sounds safe that way," he said slowly. "You sure you can deal with this rancher all right?"

"He ain't no rancher," Watts said, expanding under Slocum's look of obvious admiration. "He's a *general*," Watts went on. He pronounced the word the Spanish way. "All got up fer the circus. Big sombrero with gold thread, charro pants with silver pesos flattened out an' sewed along the seams, two ca'tridge belts crossed over his chest. An' he stinks."

"Stinks?"

"Never washes. I don't wash much, but he *never* washes."

"He's a real general?"

"Hell, no. Just a *bandido*. I c'n deal with 'im all right. Now take you, fer instance. You don't know nobody, you come in all alone. Or with them two lightweights out there. An' then someone's bound to recernize you fer the man who was with them two Mexicans who never was seen no more. An' you say you fired 'em. If you fired 'em so close to their homes, how come they ain't been back?"

Slocum knew enough by now to be able to find his contact. "You've been a great help, Mr. Watts," he said politely.

It was clear to Slocum that Watts would like very much to know what had happened to Rodolfo and Tito. Since Watts had never struck Slocum as the kind of man who went around collecting information that he could not use, he must have a good reason for wanting to know. And when he did find out, Slocum felt absolutely sure, he would use the knowledge as a weapon.

"People come an' people go," Slocum concluded, rising.

Watts shrugged, masking his irritation. "Nobody's seen 'em," he said.

Slocum held out his palms and shrugged. He put on his hat.

"I'll guess I'll go to Saragoza," he said amiably.

"You're crazy!" Watts shouted.

Slocum slowly turned and looked at Watts. His green eyes burned. He did not bandy words. Watts added, "I mean, you ain't logical, Pearson," he said, in a mollifying tone. "You gotta run rings 'round these people, get 'em confused, else they'll walk all over you. I'm tellin' you, do it my way. It sounds complicated, goin' back, an' gettin' on a train, an' gettin' off way over in Texas—but it's got a kind of logic to it."

Slocum's time as an army officer had taught him, with bitter experience, that complicated maneuvers usually fell flat. He stared at Watts. That gentleman abruptly decided to shut up. As Slocum walked out into the street, Watts moved to his window and looked out at Slocum with malevolence.

Slocum told Hannum that he would be going into Saragoza by himself. "I ought to be back by six," he said. "You and Eddie better stick by the wagon. I don't trust our friend much." Eddie gave him a sour look and resumed picking his nose.

As Slocum rode away he thought with dry amusement that the three people he had just ridden away from would all be delighted if he were to die in Saragoza that afternoon.

He smothered a chuckle. Putting his life on the line once again wasn't that important any more.

11

Several children were throwing stones at a skinny brown mongrel as Slocum rode into Saragoza. The dog walked patiently away, its tail curled between its skeletal legs and down under its belly. One stone hit it on the neck. It yelped and broke into a trot, its tail still curling in the same position. Slocum inserted his horse between the children and the dog and told them harshly to stop. They stared at him in astonishment. He waited till the dog had slipped between two low adobe houses. The resentful children stared at him as he rode on.

He dismounted in front of the *pulqueria*. It was called La Flor de Sonora. The name was painted in careful flowery scrolls above the double swinging doors which extended from shoulder to waist level of anyone walking in. A thick, old bougainvillea vine coiled above the doors, weaving in and out of a rusting iron balcony. Some of the red flowering masses swayed back and forth above the doors. He had to duck under the vine as he pushed through. He sat down at a dirty table and ordered tequila. The bartender looked as if he wished it was Slocum's throat he had under his knife as he sliced a lime with a rusty knife. He placed a small saucer of salt in front of Slocum together with the tequila and the lime slice. He stared in a hostile fashion as Slocum licked the salt, gulped the tequila, and bit deeply into the lime. The liquor went down like a red-hot poker. He ordered another one. It would never do to rush things when he wanted to find out something.

There were four men at the bar. They had all turned around and were staring at Slocum. They did not pretend that they were not staring. It was quite unlike other places where Mexicans drank. The stares were icy and calm, not surreptitious and resentful. Slocum got the feeling that they were going to make a move soon. He trusted his hunches. He immediately changed his plan. Instead of waiting inside a place full of hostile people, he would do better to be out in the open. Full sunlight would suit him better than this dark corner. And once outside, he would be sure to stick close to his horse in case it should suddenly become advisable to leave Saragoza at a fast gallop.

Then he saw several pairs of legs coming toward the swinging doors with a quick, purposeful stride. It had begun, then; much sooner than he had calculated. Quietly he eased the Colt out of his holster and placed it in his lap.

The legs stopped outside the doors. He lowered his right hand to his lap and suddenly felt a ring of steel pressed against the back of his neck. Too late, he remembered the little window that let in some light.

"*Manos arriba, hideputa!* Hands up, you son of a bitch!"

No point in being foolish. He put his hands up.

The steel pressed harder.

"*Alto, más alto!*"

He stretched them all the way, thinking of what he had once said to a stagecoach driver he was robbing. "Put 'em up so high that when I tell you to lower 'em I want to see wild goose feathers in 'em." He smiled. The bartender looked at him in amazement. This was not the way people behaved who were going to die soon. Shaking his head, the man called to the people outside the door, "Come in!"

The men came in, carrying Winchesters. One handed his carbine to another and, coming close, took Slocum's Colt. He stepped back, examined it, grunted with satisfaction, and shoved it into his belt with a smirk of pleasure. He took his carbine back, stepped to the bar, and leaned back against it. He stared at Slocum unblinkingly.

No one said anything. The steel ring was withdrawn from his neck. These were professionals, Slocum knew. He felt a grudging admiration. But it was a situation that could go sour with blinding speed. He was a *gringo* in Mexico, alone, and these people probably had a burning hatred toward all Americans.

"*Qué pasa?*" Slocum demanded, keeping his voice puzzled and calm. No one responded. Slocum shrugged and drank the last of his tequila.

He was not too alarmed. The men did not have the look of a lynch mob eager for action. He would ask for the general. When they found out that he had come to speak to that important personage, things would go better. His problem, as Slocum well knew, was to ask for the general without getting himself into trouble with the *federales*—for the federal troops might be there, searching for the general. The *federales* were merciless toward *bandidos*, especially those who entertained dreams of starting a revolution.

Slocum had calculated that when he contacted the general, that gentleman would protect him out of self-interest. His need for guns and ammunition would see to that.

More men arrived. A short, powerful man strode

through the doors. The others made way for him. He held a Colt in his hand. He pointed it at Slocum and motioned briskly for him to stand up. Slocum stood up slowly, measuring distances. The man made a small circle with the muzzle. Slocum turned around and faced the wall. He estimated that the man was not furious enough to shoot him in the back.

The man told three of the others to leave their weapons on the bar and search Slocum.

Hands went through his pockets roughly, ripping them completely open. Three silver dollars fell to the dusty floor and rolled away. His tobacco sack followed. Slocum looked out of the little window through which the first Colt had come to press against the back of his neck. He saw four women sitting on a crudely made wooden bench under an álamo tree. Three had the dark faces of Indian women. The fourth one was far more slender than the others and she had much lighter, olive-tinted complexion. Her features were classically Spanish. When she she put her *rebozo* around her shoulders and suddenly caught sight of him, she gave a start of surprise as she saw the men pointing their carbines at him inside the bar.

Slocum was used to seeing Indian women lower their eyes whenever they realized they were being observed. When he looked at the woman in the *rebozo* she did not lower her gaze. She looked at him calmly, then rose. The other women immediately stood up also. When she walked away slowly, they followed her very closely. Slocum realized that they formed some kind of an escort. Unlike the barefooted *indias,* with their dirty, callused soles, she was wearing sandals, and her feet were clean. From under her long skirt a clean petticoat peeped out—another sign that she was not an Indian.

His intrigued musings about the woman were cut short by someone tying his wrists together with a piece of rawhide. He was jerked around and roughly pushed into his chair. The short man, who was clearly the leader, came forward, pulled off Slocum's boots, and examined them.

He grunted with satisfaction. Slocum was not surprised. Like all cowmen, he spent good money for his boots and his hat—both items had to stand up under the hardest wear, and only the best were good enough.

The short man pulled Slocum out of the chair. Then he sat down in it and pulled on Slocum's boots. They fit him well. He grinned with pleasure and kicked his old *alpargatas* aside. Then he crossed his thick, muscular arms and stared at Slocum.

Slocum was sure by now that some official—probably this one, who was probably himself a sheriff or some town official—had found out that Slocum had entered Mexico in order to deal with a *bandido*. He would be questioned as to his intentions in crossing into Mexico. After a day or so, after putting a fat bribe into the hands of the fat official, he would be released. That was the way these affairs were usually handled.

The important thing was to make sure that he would not be shot during the first half hour after capture, while performing the time-honored attempt-to-escape, the traditional *ley fuga*—the law of flight. He did not see how he could escape, tied up as he was, if the fat man decided to execute the *ley fuga*, but at least he could keep his eyes and ears open.

"What are you doing here?" the man asked in Spanish.

"I'm here on business. Are you the sheriff?"

The man smiled. The crowd roared in amusement. He

turned back to Slocum. "I'm the sheriff, yes. What do you want?"

"I don't want to waste your time or mine. Where's the sheriff?"

"You don't have any time left, *amigo*. Consider me the sheriff and answer my question."

Slocum deliberately turned his back on the man. He now faced the others. One of them, with a hard expression, slowly drew his forefinger across his throat.

The short man, insulted by Slocum's turning his back on him, flushed. He rose and grabbed Slocum by the elbow and spun him around. He stopped when a voice called from outside the swinging doors, "Enough, Pablo."

Slocum was roughly shoved out into the street. One man had taken Slocum's fine felt sombrero and clapped his own ragged straw one on Slocum. It was too small, but Slocum was grateful for the protection it would give against the fierce Sonoran sun. He was shoved roughly onto his horse. He looked for the man who had called upon Pablo to stop, but whoever it was, he had disappeared. The men now stood talking in low tones. They were clearly waiting for someone to show up.

Finally a man came out of an adobe restaurant across the street. He was eating a tortilla from which black beans were dripping. He gulped everything, wiped his mouth with the back of his brown hand, and stared at Slocum with an intelligent, calculating, sour gaze. Slocum judged him to be in his middle thirties. He seemed to be deferred to by all the men present. They waited patiently for him to swallow his food.

The man stepped back into the restaurant and gave a curt order. The four women Slocum had seen earlier stepped out. In the middle, with long, easy strides, walked the girl who had earlier caught his attention. As they passed by she looked at the man with a stare of cold, calm hatred. He seemed to be waiting for it, and when he saw it he burst into laughter.

His hair was black and he needed a haircut. He wore the shaggy black mustache customary with Indians. The *mestiza* who ran the restaurant came out with a tortilla in one hand. In the other she carried a huge sombrero lavishly embroidered with gold thread. He put it on with one hand while he ate the fresh tortilla with the other. For the first time Slocum saw that the man was wearing *charro* trousers with silver pesos that had been flattened and bent to follow the natural curve of the legs.

He mounted a fine black stallion. He came alongside Slocum and, as Slocum had expected, the whiff of the man's unwashed body hit him almost like a blow.

"Oye, gringo!" he said curtly.

"I want—" Slocum began. He had started to say that he wanted to talk to the man alone about the shipment of shovels, but he had only gotten out two words when the Mexican slashed him across the face with a quirt that was attached to his wrist by a leather loop. The cut burned like a drench of acid.

"I talk, *gringo.* You listen. *Comprende?"*

"I—" Slocum began once more. He knew he had to talk fast, before someone pulled him out of the saddle and shot him. The quirt slashed again.

"You got no time to talk, *gringo,"* the man said lazily. "Me, I got time. I'm a *general.* You know what a *general* is? That's me. I'm half Yaqui, half Spanish. I can't never be no cavalry officer in the goddamn Mexican army. So I make myself my own general. Pretty good, huh?" He translated for his men, who roared with appreciative laughter.

He turned to Slocum and demanded, "Hey, how you like my English?"

"You talk better than me," Slocum said. His glance roved carefully up and down the man. A hundred yards in front the scouts rode, a hundred yards in back came the rear guard. He counted a force of about sixty. They all looked tough, tall, thin, all with the big Sonoran sombreros. All carried machetes. Perhaps one out of five carried a carbine. And of these men, Slocum saw that their cartridge belts were only a quarter full. They had an easy, professional air about them. But with that scarcity of weapons and ammunition there was no way they could fight any kind of serious battle.

"I talk better than you? I think that's very funny."

The general frowned. He lifted his quirt and thoughtfully rubbed his mustache with it. Then he chuckled. "I work three years in Texas," he said. "One day I get tired of people callin' me dirty spik. So one night I killed my foreman and come across the Rio Grande—" He clicked his tongue several times in succession and slapped each leg of his *charro* trousers several times with his quirt as he pantomimed a fast ride.

"But before that I get to know plenty big people in Texas. Hey, how you like my pants?"

He looked fondly at the rows of silver pesos. "Pretty good for an Indian, no?" he demanded. Without waiting for an answer he caressed the rounded surfaces of the pesos. "I took 'em off a *hacendado* in Chihuahua." He pantomined firing a carbine. "*A la pared, hideputa!* To the wall, you son of a bitch! Boom, boom!"

He brightened. "Same *hacienda* where my father was a *peón*. This *hacendado*, he took my sister. Oh, she was pretty. He told my father not to poke aroun' askin' what happen to her. My mother, she cry a lot, so she went to the big house to ask. He hit her with a whip. I come back fifteen years later with two hundred fifty men. My father and mother were dead, no one heard of my sister for years. I bet she was so ashamed she ran away and become a whore. I killed the *mayordomo* very quick. He didn't deserve to die so fast, but he was a very good man with a knife. I had to have quiet, no?

"I pulled the *hacendado* out of his bed. He still up to his old tricks, he had a girl, maybe she was twelve, she was in bed with him. Next morning I call all the *peones* together to watch me. His wife was dead long time ago, too bad. His daughter in a convent in Paris, too bad. At sunrise I drive my knife through both cheeks an' through his tongue because he kept sayin' bad things, real bad things, about me an' my friends. Then I made a hole in his nose and put a little chain through it an' I lead him around like a burro. Oh, he was stubborn!"

The general chuckled at the memory. "But he follow me, all right. After a while I got tired of that. Then I cut a little piece off each finger. We Yaquis very good about that. *Peones* getting bored now. Then I did other things. They not bored no more, oh my, no. After he died I say to the *peones, 'Amigos!* What you think the government do to you for not stopping me, eh? They come an' do the same to you like I did to your *patrón!* True?' I say. True, they say. So I ask, where is safety? With me, I told them. Always moving. Always with good guns, plenty bullets, when we take another *hacienda* plenty good clothes for the women, maybe good silver candlesticks from the chapel. So my army grows. It is not hard. Plenty mountains to hide in, enough *maíz,* plenty deer, plenty rocks to roll down on the *federales*.

"An' one week after I kill him, who you think

comes? His daughter! She came in a coach, with escort of six soldiers. We kill the soldiers, fast, *fast!* I got the girl. Some day I take her like her father take my sister. She don' like to wait, she don' like suspense. That's why I want her to wait. I learn one thing in my life—waitin' for a bad thing to happen is worse than if it happen right away. Ah, I see from your face you know what I'm talkin' about. *Sí, Tejano!*"

"I'm not a Texan," Slocum said.

"Don' matter—you a *gringo,* no difference. I don' know why I talk to you so much. Maybe because you got *cojones,* comin' here alone, a *Tejano, por Dios!* An' after what you done."

Slocum didn't like the way the general's voice suddenly lost its easy amiability and slid into that menacing last sentence. He pretended that it had no special meaning as far as he was concerned. But from the level, savage stare the man was giving him from under the wide brim of his sombrero, Slocum knew that his life was hanging from a very thin thread. The general had pronounced that last sentence slowly and heavily, as if he were a judge announcing a verdict.

"You kill two Mexicans last time you was down here," the general added. "I'm gonna take three, maybe four days to kill you. I don' want no arguments, no talk. *Comprende?* Finish."

He rode ahead. His golden sombrero stood out among the other plain ones.

Ten minutes later they came to a little muddy river with steep banks. Slocum's horse hesitated a moment, and Pablo lashed her flanks with his quirt. She leaped sideways, kicking wildly at Pablo's horse. She fell on her side and slithered to the shallow bottom, pressing Slocum into the foot-thick mud. His head was under the surface of the mud. He held his breath. Pablo chuckled as the mare slipped and struggled, trying to stand erect. Each time she fell she pressed Slocum's head deeper into the mud. Since the mud was thick, he was not hurt when the mare's weight fell on him, but it took all his will to keep from yelling for help. The general looked on, amused.

The captured girl suddenly leaped off her horse and into the mud. She grabbed Slocum's head and pulled it out of the mud, heedless of the filth that covered her skirts and legs. Slocum had just enough time to gasp his thanks when the general put his horse into the water and slashed her face with his doubled-up riata. She tried to grab the riata but he held it aloft and laughed, whirling it around and around his head while he fended her off easily with his own hand. Slocum set his teeth in helpless rage. Then he began to vomit the water and mud he had swallowed while the horse was rolling on him.

The horse scrambled erect. Slocum was shoved roughly into the saddle. Pablo pulled out Slocum's carbine, wiped the mud from it, looked at it lovingly, looked warily at the general, and reluctantly thrust it back into the saddle scabbard. Slocum was sure that the general must have earmarked the gun for himself. It was a new one, and the bright brass must have had a strong attraction for the general. Slocum bent over and vomited again.

After a minute of retching he lifted his head. He saw the girl riding in the middle of her female escort while they slapped and shoved her. She refused to wince or to turn aside from the blows. Even in his nausea Slocum began to admire the cool arrogance with which she flaunted her indifference to her muddy clothes and the red welts on her face.

•   •   •

Two hours later Slocum recognized where he was. A month before he had made his night camp with Tito and Rodolfo very close to this road. The air smelled bad. Slocum was jerked off his horse and propelled roughly through the chaparral. He saw the ring of stones which marked the old campfire. There was the square-shaped flat stone on which he rested his feet while he ate. He had rolled himself in his blanket nearby. And there, close to the *cholla*, was where he had heard the dry clicks of the Winchester as the cartridge was levered into the chamber. Twenty feet further on was where he had dragged their bodies and stripped them for the *zapilotes*.

"You don' like the smell? That's too bad," the general said as he looked at Slocum's face. "Get off."

Slocum had never dismounted from a horse with his wrists tied behind his back. He hesitated for a second, trying to figure out how to do it. The general spurred his horse and the impact of the heavy stallion against Slocum's slightly built mare sent him sprawling off on the far side. One spur caught in the stirrup. His horse had started to shy away from what it had obviously thought was a crazy mount. But it was well trained, and stopped as soon as it realized that its rider's spur was caught.

Slocum lay helpless on his back, looking straight up into the sky. He had been in a lot of tight places in his time, but this one looked hopeless. He was beginning to feel a sense of panic. He felt quite sure that there was nothing that could deter the general from his passion for revenge for all the indignities he had suffered across the river in the States, and for the revenge he felt he must take from Slocum for the two murdered men.

As Slocum lay on his back, with his ankle twisted in the stirrup, he was trying to think how he could possibly persuade the general that he had killed the two men in self-defense. Under his huge sombrero, the general's hard brown face stared down at him.

A woman's hand reached into Slocum's upside-down angle of vision. It pulled his ankle out of the stirrup. He struggled to a sitting position and stared up into her blue eyes. It was the same woman who had helped him at the river. In every way she showed the strain of the *Conquistadores*—the way she held her head high with an unconscious serene arrogance, her stately walk, and the bone structure of her face. Only the olive complexion and the blue-black lights of her hair recalled her part-Indian heritage. With her blue eyes for contrast she was one of the most striking and beautiful women Slocum had ever seen.

Slocum managed to struggle to his feet. He stood, feet thrust wide apart in the red trail in the ocean of the dusty gray chapparal. The general was sitting cross-legged on the ground with his carbine across his knees, watching Slocum intently.

"*Tejano*, you don' like me?" he demanded. He chuckled, lit a cigarette, and motioned. One of the *bandidos* brought up a pick and shovel and threw them at Slocum's feet. The general looked around at the ground critically, like an artist deciding where to begin his canvas.

"I think there," he said. He pointed to the stony soil with a dirty forefinger. Then he leaned back and said, "We are waitin', *amigo*."

Slowly Slocum began to dig.

"Tell me," the general asked curiously, "why don' you cover them with rocks, eh? No coyotes. No *zapilotes*.

Nobody finds 'em. *Tejano,*" he finished, shaking his head in mock despair, "you *estúpido,* no?"

Slocum silently agreed. He had thought the *zapilotes* would rapidly dispose of the bodies, as they usually did. Perhaps the ones in the area had been well fed and just let this lot go. He had not been in any mood to spend an hour or more carrying rocks back and forth, lest someone should notice him and wonder what he was up to. Almost everywhere, even in the most obviously uninhabited places, he had come across narrow little trails. It was clear enough now that he should have simply wasted that hour picking up stones, even at the risk of being discovered by a lonely *peón* trudging by.

He dismissed the regret from his mind. He dug slowly and carefully, thinking hard. He was becoming very thirsty as he picked away at the hard-packed soil in the glare of the open sun. Without his sombrero, the sweat ran into his eyes. The salt burned. From time to time, he straightened up and wiped his face with his sleeve.

"You got a good grave," observed the general genially. "I like the way you dig. Nice square corners." Slocum squatted and rubbed dirt onto his palms for a better grip on the pick.

The general said, "Your good frien' Señor Watts sent me a message las' night." Slocum stared at him, arranging his face into a look of polite curiosity, although he did not like the sound of the remark.

"He tol' me where to find you. Aha, Pablo! Look at him! I tol' he don' like that!"

Slocum tried to make his face impassive.

"Watts has been very used—no, useful to me. We are good—friends is not the word. No. We do business together. You think, if I kill you how will I get my Winchesters? Eh? *Verdad, hombre?*"

"That's just what I'm thinking," Slocum said. "Because you are *not* going to get 'em. Not from Watts, you're not."

"*Porqué?*" asked the general, with a wide grin.

"*Porque* Watts is goin' to do what George Sheridan wants, even though he don't like him. He's not stupid."

The general's smile grew wider as he translated for Pablo. Then he turned and asked, "So?"

"So," Slocum said, "the only way you can get your Winchesters is to send me back." He leaned on his pick. He had dug one foot of the grave, and his face, from the unaccustomed exposure without a hat, was seared a dull red.

The general looked at him slowly, up and down, savoring the moment.

"*Hombre,*" he said, "I don' have to do nothin'. *Comprende?* You come down to Mexico, you go in alone to a Sonoran town, you got *cojones* all right, but when you get killed no one cares, *verdad?* Watts sees you don' come back. He finds out you been killed. So he takes the Winchesters an' *he* makes a deal with me. The way Sheridan wants it. So wha' happen then? Sheridan says, well, poor Señor Pearson, nex' time I go down Saragoza way maybe I drop some roses into the river for him, or maybe I even buy some candles in the church for him. Oh, he dunno I'm gonna plant you in a grave. Tha's somethin' you don' deserve, but you got *cojones,* hombre, that I do for you."

He stood up suddenly, struck by a new idea. Thrusting his carbine high in the air and shaking it in his enthusiasm, he said, "An' one more thing! You wan' to write a letter to your mother, I let you! I see it gets mailed across the river, you don' have to worry about no Mexican post office."

One of the men had been busily hacking branches off a mesquite. Using rawhide thongs, he had made three crude crosses. He tossed them at the head of the grave.

"See, *amigo*," said the general, "I like you. You get one. I ain't no Apache."

Slocum dug on stubbornly. He plotted his last maneuver. At the last moment, he planned to make his attack. He didn't think he would escape, not with all those armed men carefully watching him, but it would be better to get killed fighting than to be shot like a steer destined for the table. Slocum threw out another shovelful.

"Smooth, very good," the general observed with approval. "I like the way you do it!" He sliced a palm vertically. "No hurry. I wan' a good grave for them two vaqueros you shot in the back."

Slocum lifted his sweat-soaked face. His sombrero had floated off down the river when his horse had slipped in the mud. "Never shot anyone in the back," he said quietly, and resumed digging.

"Sure, *hombre*. Sure. Hole plenty deep, *amigo*."

For ten minutes more Slocum dug. His clothes were drenched with sweat. When he had the sides of the grave as squared off and smooth as he could make them, he straightened up.

"Finish?"

"Finished," Slocum said.

The general stood up and threw away his cigarette. He pumped a cartridge into the chamber of his carbine. Several men, lounging in the shade of a mesquite, sat up and crossed themselves.

"Out!" said the general, motioning with the muzzle of the carbine.

Slocum climbed out and stretched. He nodded toward

the cigarette the general had just discarded and asked, "How about a fresh one for me?"

"Sure," the general said. He liked Slocum's display of cool unconcern. He reached into a pocket and pulled out a tobacco sack and cigarette paper. Slocum knew this was his last chance, the one he had been waiting for. He began to walk toward the general with his arm extended. When he got within range, he intended to leap for the carbine.

"No, *chico,* no," said the general, almost regretfully, Slocum thought. He swung the muzzle toward Slocum's heart. Then he thrust a match and a cigarette paper inside the tobacco sack and tossed it to Slocum. Slocum shrugged. His last chance had vanished. He made his cigarette, lit it, and decided that it would be useless to try to walk toward the general once more to return the sack. He grinned and tossed the sack to the man, who caught it and grinned back.

Slocum smoked the cigarette slowly as he stood alone in the chaparral.

Suddenly the general asked, "Do you believe in God?"

"Not especially," Slocum said. He took a long drag.

"What is 'especially'?" asked the general in a displeased tone.

"I mean—" Slocum began. He decided he could not define the word, and that the problem of defining it just then was something he didn't care about. "Oh, hell," he said. "Just say the answer is no."

The general looked shocked. "Me," he said seriously, "I believe in God. But I don' wan' to go to heaven. Heaven is for the stinkin' rich Mass-goers in Durango or Chihuahua. I wan' to go where a man like Juarez went. Tell me, *Tejano,* where did Juarez go?"

Slocum let smoke dribble from his nostrils. He
shrugged. *"Quién sabe?"* he said, and threw his butt
away.

"All right," the general said, all business. "Stan' in
the grave. No funny business, *amigo. Ándale!"*

Slocum did not move.

"The grave, *cabrón!"*

Slocum did not move. He stared at the general. One
thing was absolutely sure in his mind: he would not cooper-
ate in his death. The general spoke a sentence in Spanish so quickly that Slocum did not catch it. Several men
put down their carbines and took off their gun belts.
They took off their knives and set them on the ground.
Then they moved toward him from every direction.

Slocum waited on the balls of his feet, his hands half
clenched. It would be six to one. Two men came to the
edge of the grave opposite him. They started to step
down into it. They dropped their eyes for a fraction of a
second. Slocum had been waiting for that: he jumped
quickly into the grave and jerked an ankle out from
under each man. They were sent sprawling, but three
more men had launched themselves at him from the rear.
He had expected that, and he was ready; he fought with
fists and teeth and elbows.

In two seconds two men were half paralyzed from
blows into their solar plexuses. They were doubled
over; one man held his nose, from which blood was
pouring. From the corner of one eye Slocum saw that the
general was watching the fray with not a sign of alarm.
He even lifted his cigarette for a puff, with a look of
amused interest. It gave Slocum the feeling that he was
simply supplying the general with a brief, amusing interlude
for the day. Nevertheless, Slocum fought on, panting in
the heat like a dog. Two man ran up; one had a Colt

stuck in his belt. Slocum saw it, but before he could make a move for the gun two arms went around his neck from the rear. He broke the grip by falling on his knees and bending forward. He fought erect and lunged at the man with the Colt.

A riata dropped over his head and tightened on his upper arms. He tried to work it loose; another riata dropped over his head, tightened across his chest, and jerked him sideways to the bottom of the grave. He struggled to his knees and started to rise when a third riata settled around his neck and tightened. A roar like a waterfall filled his ears. He fell back, unconscious.

12

As Slocum struggled upward to consciousness he heard the sound of a hammer. He had been propped up against a mesquite trunk. His elbows were bound to his sides and a rawhide thong cut deeply into his wrists. Someone had spilled water on it and the leather had shrunk so much that his hands felt numb. The general had not budged. His carbine was still across his lap.

Slocum's throat felt sore. He swallowed what little saliva he could produce from his dry mouth. His throat hurt badly when he swallowed. The hammering went on. He turned his head. His saddle lay upside down on the ground, and a man was hammering spikes into the cantle so that the points stuck two inches beyond its leather cover. The wooden saddle tree held the spikes firmly in place.

The general noticed immediately that Slocum was conscious. He looked with a wide grin at Slocum's bewildered stare. The business with the saddle seemed pointless to Slocum, but he craved water so badly that he dismissed the saddle from his mind. When he turned his head the effort made him groan; his whole body was badly bruised.

The general nodded. The saddle blanket and the saddle were thrown onto the horse and cinched. Four men sat Slocum into the saddle. He leaned forward to escape the pressure of the nail points against the small of his back. By arching his back to his maximum he found that the points just grazed the base of his spine.

One of the men now mounted and tied his riata to the reins of Slocum's horse. Then they all moved a quarter of a mile down the road, where there was a wide, flat area. When they reached it the man leading Slocum's horse paused and looked at the general, who was busily thrusting several cartridges into his carbine until it was full.

Then he nodded. At the end of thirty feet of riata Slocum's horse was obediently trotting. At the general's nod, the man spurred his horse. By the time he had reached a fast trot, the arch of Slocum's back could not protect him any more. He was bouncing too much, and the sawing movement was raking his skin. He tried to lean forward. The general lifted his carbine.

Slocum hoped that the bullet would kill him quickly. He did not want to be dragged through the chaparral, wounded, hanging by one foot from the stirrup. He braced for the shock of the bullet.

The crack of the Winchester in the desert air sounded flat and without menace, almost like a cheap firecracker. Its passage not six inches from his face pushed the air against his cheek. He saw the general grin as he ejected the shell. He had missed deliberately, Slocum knew, and that took as much skill as hitting him while he was in motion.

"*Pronto!*" yelled the general to the rider. "*Más pronto!*"

The vaquero broke from his fast trot into a gallop. It did Slocum no good to lean forward to try to escape from the spikes. The speed at which he was now moving was grinding the points viciously against his lower back.

Once more the general fired. This time the bullet passed a few inches in back of Slocum's head. Slocum realized that the man were judging his distances in order to miss him closely. He would be killed if he were to move his head a few inches to the front or to the rear. He would have to remain in one position—and that with the spikes digging into his back.

The game went on for ten more minutes. Pablo was allowed to fire a few shots. Then the general tired of the game. Three men tore Slocum roughly from the saddle. The pain in his spine was agonizing.

Pablo drew his machete and ran his thumb along the edge gently. A thin red hairline cut appeared on his dirty, callused skin. He held up his bleeding thumb, grinned, and ran the thin red streak across his throat.

Slocum was half dragged, half carried to a cotton-wood branch lying on the ground beside a dried-up *arroyo*. Its top had been carved by the men's machetes until it was V-shaped. He was made to stand barefoot on the sharp top edge. Three of the men held him while two others, using their combined strength, pulled his legs as far apart as they could until Slocum was sure that the tendons would crack. Then they lashed his feet securely to the branch with rawhide thongs.

His wrists were still tied behind his back. A riata was tied to the lashing and thrown over a branch of the cottonwood. Two men pulled down on the riata. The strain on his back and shoulder muscles caused intense pain. His shoulder blades were forced into close contact, pressing the vertebrae inwards. Wave after wave of excruciating agony flowed from the base of his spine, where his flesh had been severely lacerated by the spikes.

In this position, Slocum's head was bent forward. A

hand grabbed his hair and jerked his head up. The general bent down and looked at Slocum with mock solicitude.

"You all right, *Tejano?*" he asked. "You sick, mebbe?"

Slocum looked up at him. His face was impassive, but his green eyes blazed with silent fury. He said nothing. After a moment, the general let Slocum's head drop back on his chest.

"Don' worry, *Tejano,*" the general went on, "you come to Mexico to see me, I give you somethin' to look at."

Another hand grabbed Slocum's hair and snapped his head backward. He felt a wave of heat pulsating from something—for a moment he thought it was the sun, since it came from directly overhead.

Then he saw. It was a white-hot branding iron. Pablo was holding it, rolling back and forth.

"This one is hot, *Tejano,*" the general said. He bent down, picked up a dried twig, and touched it to the iron. It shriveled to a twisted gray ash and a wisp of acrid smoke drifted up.

Slocum saw that the brand was LIPM.

"Libertad y Independencia Para México," the general remarked proudly. "My brand. For my cattle. First political cattle brand! You come to Mexico to see what business you could do with me, no? I show you. With *Libertad y Independencia* I close your eyes." He motioned to Pablo.

Pablo grinned and raised the iron. Slowly he moved the white-hot letters closer and closer. He finally stopped it one inch from Slocum's eyes.

Slocum squeezed his eyes as tightly shut as he could. The heat was so intense that his eyeballs felt as dry as an alkali flat. His nose felt as if it were on fire.

Time seemed to run on and on, but the whole thing lasted less than thirty seconds. The heat went away. The hand released his hair, and his head fell forward. When he lifted his aching, inflamed eyelids he saw everything through a red haze. His left eye ached and throbbed, and every few seconds it seemed as if something passed in front of it, darkening his vision. He thought for a moment that someone was holding a hand in front of his eye deliberately, but then he realized that no one was there.

With his right eye he could see fairly well, except that everything seemed red instead of its usual color. The hot iron had been thrown down on the ground and was sizzling a few paces in front of him.

Slocum's horse had been tied to an ocotillo branch near him. It was nibbling at the crimson flowers of the ocotillo, unconcerned with what was happening to Slocum. Through the red blur which was almost the whole of Slocum's sight he saw Pablo as he pulled the Winchester from Slocum's saddle scabbard. It had been lying in the sun, and the mud which had oozed inside the muzzle when his horse had slipped into the river had dried as hard as adobe by now. When Pablo had the gun out of the scabbard, he hefted it with pleasure. He liked the weight and the balance and he was so stupid, Slocum saw, that he did not notice the mud that had plugged up the barrel.

Pablo pumped a cartridge into the chamber. He hefted it once more. *"Para mí, mi general?"* he asked ingratiatingly.

The general nodded. Pablo nestled the stock against his cheek and pointed the carbine to the harsh blue sky. He squeezed the trigger.

The muzzle burst. The carbine turned a somersault in

the air. Pablo fell back to the ground. He remained on his back, bleeding badly from his face, screaming like a child. His nose was broken, one eye was gone, and several of his front teeth were shattered. He held both dirty hands to his face, writhing and kicking at the men who were trying to pull the hands away. Slocum smiled at the sight: his gun had punished one of his torturers.

The general looked at him. "You like it, *Tejano*?" he said slowly. "Tomorrow we see if you still laugh. *Buenas noches.*"

13

"This Mr. Watts," said Eddie, looking between the breasts of the girl who was sitting in his lap. "This here Mr. Watts," he repeated. The yellow glare of the kerosene lantern hanging on a hook on the whorehouse wall made the girl look almost pretty.

"Yeah," Sam Hannum said, lifting his fifth full glass of bourbon.

"This Mr. Watts," Eddie said with finality, rubbing the girl's naked shoulder with his unshaven jaw until she winced and angrily tried to shake him off.

"Spit it out!" Hannum said. He set his glass down carefully. "Spit it out, goddamn it! I dunno, but I can't drink no more till you spit it out. You're curryin' that gal like she's a horse, you dang fool."

Eddie stood up abruptly. The girl slid between his legs to the floor. "*Hideputa!*" she screamed.

Eddie went out. He stumbled from table to chair to wall to door. After a minute he returned, staggered inside, and fell into his chair again. The girl sat promptly in his lap once more and squeezed his neck in an embrace.

"Where'd-ja go?"

"Where the hell didja think I went?" Eddie said, without heat. He filled another glass and said, "This Mr. Watts is suttinly good to us, ain't he?"

"On the house, he said," Sam stated. He waved his

glass in a grand gesture and spilled it over his girl's dress. She jumped up and screamed in rage. Then she backed against the wall and wrung out her skirt, simmering in anger. She ran out of the room.

"These Mex girls git excited easy," Sam said. "Bourbon on the house! Gals on the house!"

"Yeah, tha's right," said Eddie. "He's real nice. But you ain't nice. I ain't nice. What I mean is, why should he be nice to us? Hey?"

"Aw, shuddup an' drink. Worry 'bout it in the mornin'. All by yourself. I'll be all cuddled up with a hangover."

"No. Le's worry 'bout it *now*. Pearson didn't come back by sundown. Right?"

"Right!"

"So somethin' musta happened. Right?"

"Sonabitch is dead. Le's celebrate. Le's celebrate free!"

"Yeah. Le's celebrate. But first y' better think, Sam."

"Why do I gotta think?"

Eddie said to his girl, "Speak English, baby?"

"No. Me no spik Eenglish."

"Sure," Eddie said cynically. "Y' go downstairs an' git us more whisky, all right?" He gave her a silver dollar. "This is all fer you, *mamita,* and not fer the *señora.*"

She grinned with pleasure and left. "So why do I gotta think?" repeated Hannum impatiently.

"Thought I'd take a look at our shovels while I was out there takin' a leak. Overheard a couple of Watts's boys talkin'. I know where Pearson is."

"Where's the bastard? Spread-eagled out in the cactus?"

"Just about. He's tied up pretty good. Those Mexicans know how. He ain't in very good condition. Seems he ain't gonna last long.''

"Best news I heard since Abe Lincoln got kilt! Have a drink.''

"It was Mr. Watts who fixed it all.''

"Hope Pearson roasts in hell on a gridiron made o' Yankee skeletons. A toast to Watts!''

"I saw somethin' else,'' Eddie went on relentlessly.

"Ain't you the little gossiper tonight. Where the hell did that gal go?'' He stood and walked to the edge of the staircase and peered downstairs.

Eddie caught his elbow and hissed in his ear. "Our wagon's gettin' emptied.''

"Our wagon's empty, we'll worry 'bout that in the mornin'. *Señorita! Venga!*''

"It's also George Sheridan's wagon. An' he ain't gonna like this at all. *At all*.''

Sam Hannum finally realized what Eddie was saying. "Y' mean Watts ain't such a great guy? That what you mean?''

"That's what I mean.''

Hannum leaned against the wall for support and put his hand on his gun butt. "Jesus,'' he breathed. "We better git goin'.''

"Hold it!''

"Why hold it?'' yelled Sam. "George Sheridan'll pull my guts out an' wrap 'em around a stepladder when we tell 'im!''

"That's why we gotta hold it, you goddamn fool!''

Watts stuck his head into the room. "Any trouble, boys?'' he asked.

"Nope,'' Eddie said. "He's jus' tellin' me a story an' he likes to act it out. Now you siddown, Sam, you're actin' up a mite too much.''

"Good story?"

"I like it."

"Like to see you boys havin' fun. Where's the girl?"

"Went out to fetch us more whiskey."

"You want another one, just say the word. I want you boys to have yourselves a real good time. You had a hard trip down here." He withdrew.

"I'm tellin' you he's smart," Eddie said quietly. "Y' better talk quiet, or you will *really* get your guts wound around a stepladder. You gonna listen?"

"Go on," Sam said sullenly.

"The only way you an' me are gonna come out of this without Cousin George usin' that ol' stepladder is to git someone smart 'round here to run things."

"You snot-nosed kid—"

"Because," Eddie went on impatiently, "there's only one guy smart enough 'round here to finish the deal. You know who. An' Sheridan likes him too. When Cousin George finds out that we had a chance to save Pearson's ass an' we didn't try—man, I tell you we better start headin' south an' not stop. You want to ask Watts for a cut out of the deal he's workin' an' then ride for Tierra del Fuego?"

Sam was silent.

"Well?"

"You know I got a wife an' two kids," Sam muttered.

Eddie stood up and waited.

Sam stood. "I don't like to agree with you," he said. "Goddamn you, you little needle-nosed punk, how we gonna find 'im in the dark out there? We don' know this goddamn country!" His face was full of worried tension. The girl came back with a bottle and set it down on the table.

"Nice legs, huh?" said Sam, brightening.

"Tell 'er you're gonna take a leak," Eddie said. Sam pantomimed the action. She nodded and the two men walked out, sobering rapidly.

They neared the stable quietly. Two men were handing the gun crates down to a third, who was busily stacking them into another wagon. Watts was leaning against a wall under a lantern and checking off the cases on a sheet of paper.

"Put 'em up," Eddie said. "Better hurry up," he added. "I'm drunk an' I might squeeze this here hair trigger an' not mean it. Against the wall, all of you. Sam, pull out their guns. An' you better not try to use 'im to cover yourselves an' try fer a shot at me, neither."

"Look here," said Watts. He was surprised at Eddie's coolness and obvious competence with the Colt in his steady right hand. "You men are just cuttin' yourselves a big hunk of trouble. And after I treated you so good!" He shook his head at their ingratitude.

Sam threw the men's guns under the wagon seat. "Mr. Watts," he said thickly, "I'm dumb an' I know it." He held on to the side of the wagon for support. "But I don't like to be treated like I'm dumb. It makes me feel like I'm *really* dumb. It makes me mad," he added, becoming red-faced with annoyance and waving his Colt muzzle back and forth.

The four men against the wall stared at the muzzle as if they were paralyzed.

"So shut up!" Sam bellowed.

"They're shut up," Eddie said. "For crissakes, stop yellin'!"

"O.K.," Sam said, mollified. He leaned against the wagon and belched. He closed his eyes. After a second he opened them again. "What we come in for?" he demanded of Eddie. "We musta come in here for somethin'."

"To get our guns back," Eddie said patiently.

"O.K.," Sam said with brisk efficiency. "Fust thing I want you guys to do—what's the fust thing they gotta do, Eddie?"

"Oh, jeez," Eddie said. "Sam, move back. Mr. Watts, why don' you an' your men load up that wagon again?"

Eddie sat on a bale of hay with his Colt on his lap and watched. In five minutes the wagon was full once more.

"Hitch up the team," he said. "Saddle up our horses. An' we're gonna rent one o' your saddle horses, an' a saddle."

"You're stealin' 'em," Watts said. "I got witnesses. You'll hang."

"No, we won't," Eddie said. "Uncle George will pay. Now all you guys lie down on your bellies."

"Do me a favor," Eddie said. "Put that Colt away. I don' want it goin' off in my ear on this lousy road."

"Think they'll stay tied up long?" asked Sam as he shoved the Colt back in its holster.

"They'll work loose by sunup, I bet."

"What we gonna do next?"

"We better hide this goddamn wagon an' git someone smart. When the sun is up they'll be all over like fleas on a Mex dog."

"They're gonna find us too!"

"Aw, shut up. This here road's sandy. It won't show wheel tracks much. We'll cut off somewheres and hide it in the chaparral. They'll think we went bawlin' back to George an' they'll keep on goin'. Keep your eyes peeled fer a nice little cut-off.''

They found one in the next five minutes, and swung off the road. Eddie got down and smoothed out the wheel ruts and hoofmarks they had made turning in. Five minutes later he pulled the wagon into a dense stand of mesquite. A Yaqui could have tracked them easily, but not Mexican riders in a hurry.

"That'll hold," Eddie said, satisfied. He threw the spare saddle over the spare horse and, mounting, turned to Sam.

"Ready?" he asked.

"Yeah. Ready. But not willin'.''

14

Slocum was sure he was going to die. He had been hanging in the same position all night. As dawn approached, the air became even more chilly. Numbness had crept along his arms and legs until he had the peculiar sensation of possessing a living head on a dead body. From time to time, feeling returned in an agonizing manner.

Breathing was painful in his position. The extreme retraction of his upper arms had tightened his chest muscles. It was very hard to expand his lungs against that savage pressure.

He began to shiver uncontrollably. He was wearing nothing but a thin, torn shirt and a pair of jeans. His guard had wrapped himself in a wool serape and was huddled close to his tiny fire. The fire was too far away for even the faintest glimmer of warmth to reach Slocum. From time to time the guard rose and tested Slocum's bonds; when he was satisfied that they were still tight, he sat down and wrapped himself in his serape again.

Two large hands went around the guard's neck. When he had stopped struggling, part of his shirt was ripped off and shoved into his mouth. Then the sleeve was torn off and used to hold the gag tightly in place. Next his arms and legs were tied. It was very efficiently done. Slocum stared, but in the darkness he could see very little. The guard was set up into his old position, the serape placed around him, the sombrero placed on his head; to the casual passerby he would look as if he were still on watch.

At the same time, the riata holding Slocum's arms in the air was sliced through. His body sagged, but two strong arms were holding him. A knife slashed twice and his legs were free. He could not yet stand, and when the two mysterious men put his arms around their shoulders he almost screamed aloud with the pain in the already viciously stretched tendons.

One of the men whispered hoarsely, "The son of a bitch can't walk!"

"I *know* he can't walk, y' dumb bastard," the other man replied.

"What worries me," Eddie went on, "is the way they strung 'im up all night. C'n he hold the goddamn reins? That's what worries me. Because when they find out, we better be makin' good time. They'll be madder'n a wet grizzly with cubs an' no Rio Cuajaran is gonna stop 'em."

They were silent until they reached the horses, a quarter of a mile away in the chaparral. One was a gray. On its right flank was a brand. Against the light color of the horse the dark brand stood out: Big S.

"Eddie?" Slocum asked, unbelieving.

"Shuddup," hissed Eddie. He asked venomously, "C'n y' ride?"

"Don't think so. Can't close my hands."

Eddie cursed for a moment.

"Ain'tcha got no more sense than that?" mumbled Sam under his breath. "You'll have them *bandidos* down on us with all that bellyachin'."

"For crissake," Eddie said, almost in a moan, "the bastard is gonna fall off, an' they'll pick us off like ripe berries offen a bush. Jesus, we *tried*. Let's shove off while we still got a chance.''

"He coulda rotted on that log back there like a mushroom, for all I care. But we gotta bring 'im back,'' Sam said. "Help me instead o' cryin' like a baby.'' He boosted Slocum on his stomach, then threw one of Slocum's legs viciously over the saddle horn. The strain on his already stretched tendons was more than he could bear, and he let out an involuntary gasp.

"Stop the yellin','' Eddie said. "I knew you was yeller.''

Slocum put his face against the mare's neck. It was the only way he could remain conscious. In his exhaustion and agony he bit his thumb to keep from passing out when he felt Sam lashing his legs together under the horse's belly.

A wind blew from the general's remuda toward their three horses. Sam's horse lifted her head, sniffed the air, and whinnied. Two stallions whinnied in response.

"Holy Christ!'' Eddie said, and slapped the horse on her muzzle.

"Leave my horse alone!''

"She'll git us kilt!'' Eddie wailed. "Tie him on good, an' let's get outta here!''

Shouts came from the direction of the camp.

"Help me, you little squirt!''

The two of them pressed Slocum forward till he lay flat against the horse's neck. They lashed him to the saddle horn. Some of the loops went across his spine where he had been gouged by the spikes. He bit his lips to prevent any outcry.

They trotted out into the trail. Enough light now came from the east for Slocum to see them clearly. Both were unshaven, and it was clear to him that the two of them would much rather be elsewhere. They returned Slocum's stare with irritation.

The sun was a huge red ball, free of the horizon now. It was climbing quickly. It was going to be another broiling hot day.

"Man, let's go!" Eddie said fervently. He went first, holding the reins of Slocum's horse, at a fast trot. Hearing yells from the rear, he broke into a gallop. Sam followed, his carbine already out of its scabbard. The three horses pounded hard toward the Rio Cuajaran, the border river, four miles away. The noise from the rear became clearer, and now they could hear the hoofbeats.

Slocum knew that his dead weight against its neck was slowing his horse. Eddie kept cursing and pulling hard on the reins, as if he believed that would make Slocum's horse go faster. Sam slashed the horse's hindquarters with a doubled-up riata. The sound of hooves from the rear came closer.

The horses were lathered with foam and were slowing down, but they were only three hundred yards from the Cuajaran. The Mexicans had moved up so that they were the same distance behind.

The sun was now well above the horizon. Sam's horse suddenly began to buck. It had been shot in the left buttock. He sawed desperately at the reins and managed to force it toward the river, firing several shots to the rear as he did so. The shots made their pursuers scatter from the trail, but Sam's horse, crazed with pain, began to plunge sideways and suddenly stumbled.

Sam landed on all fours. They could hear shouts of triumph from the Mexicans. But they had only a hundred feet to go. Sam grabbed hold of Eddie's stirrup and was pulled along in great leaps. The horses plunged in at a run and began swimming. The current carried them downstream, but the horses were swimming strongly. Three-quarters of the way across, the first Mexican rider appeared.

They did not have enough sense to dismount and fire from a prone position, Slocum saw. They kept firing from the nervous, shifting platforms of their panting horses. More men arrived and began firing wildly.

In a minute the Americans' horses felt bottom. They plunged up the gently sloping bank into Arizona. The firing slackened and stopped.

Slocum heard a familiar voice call across the river.

"Oye, gringo!"

Eddie untied Slocum and he slid painfully from his horse and stood up shakily.

Across the river in Mexico the general sat his horse, one hand on his left hip, the other holding the butt of the carbine on his thigh. Slocum felt dizzy and nauseated. He held on to the horn with both hands and faced Mexico.

"What do you want?" he asked.

The general beckoned him to Mexico with a sweep of his left hand. He said pleasantly, "Come on over, friend, and let's have a little talk. We're friends, aren't we?"

Slocum simply shook his head. He felt too weak to trust his voice. He could wait for his little talk—and it was one which he would do his best to make the general regret.

"No?" the general asked, with mock amazement. *"Qué lástima!"*

He turned to his men and told them that the *gringo*, for reasons which escaped him, was rejecting their warm offer of hospitality. They roared with laughter. He turned again and faced Slocum.

"*Adiós!*" he called out cheerfully.

"Tell the bastard it's not *adiós*," whispered Slocum to Eddie, "it's *hasta la vista*."

"Tell 'im yourself," Eddie said.

Slocum straightened up, though the effort cost him plenty. He knew his voice would not carry across the river. Everything swam in a red haze. He was not sure which of the blurred figures was the general.

He lifted the middle finger of his right hand in a gesture of obscene derision.

The general roared with laughter, took off his sombrero, bowed with exaggerated politeness, and waved his sombrero toward Mexico. The men around him melted into the chaparral.

15

Slocum woke up again. He had been passing out and waking up over and over again. He realized that he was no longer tied to a horse. He realized also, in a vague way, that he was not thirsty any more. Then he dropped off to unconsciousness again without knowing that an old Mexican woman had been placing a water-soaked rag in the corner of his mouth.

Once more he came to. He was lying on his stomach on a mattress made of burlap stuffed with corn shucks. It was late in the afternoon. He was naked. The old woman was placing something wet, cool, and soothing on his wrenched shoulders and lower back. His left eye still throbbed painfully, although the red haze had almost disappeared.

"Y' feel all right?" a voice asked.

Slocum started to roll to the left to look at his questioner. His spine stabbed with agony.

"Better." He stared at the big mass in the dim light of the adobe hut.

"Yeah, I'll bet," Sam said dryly. "Ever' time I started to talk t' you so far you up an' fainted like a girl. If you're gonna do it again, tell me now. I don' wanna waste m' breath."

"Feel fine. Talk."

"All right. Lemme tell y' right now. We come to help you fer one reason—we'd ketch hell from George

115

if we didn't. Fer my part, I don' give a good goddamn what they did t' you. I bet you deserved it. Eddie feels the same way, don'tcha, Eddie?''

Eddie grunted assent. Slocum said nothing. It was annoying to have had his life saved by two men he thoroughly disliked, and who disliked doing it as well. Still, it had its elements of humor. He smiled.

"We figger," Sam said brusquely, "that if Watts could fix a foxy grandpa like you he could go to town all over us. An' we'd never know what hit us till it was all over. By then George Sheridan would be sittin' on top of a barrel of rattlesnakes with us two inside."

"Where are we?"

"Dunno. We took one look at you when we untied you, an' we jus' stopped at the fust place we saw. We tol' 'em you was knocked unconscious by a low branch in the dark an' then your hoss dragged you a bit an' then we found you."

Slocum held up his swollen wrists. "How'd you explain these?"

"She din't ask, we ain't tellin', an' we tol' her we'd pay 'er plenty. Here comes her old man now."

An old Mexican with skin the color of leather was tying his burro to a branch of the cottonwood outside. He eyed them shrewdly.

"We sent 'im t' town fer medicine," Sam said.

"How do you know he won't talk?"

"We don't know," Eddie said. "But we're lucky with these people. That general crossed the river over here last year and killed all his goats an' barbecued them an' shot the old man's nephew fer tryin' to collect. I tol' him we're here to fight the general, so he's our friend. Besides, we're on top of a little ridge here, and the old guy's sheep got the ground clipped real close so no one kin creep up on us too easy."

Slocum nodded. Eddie was much smarter than he had thought at the beginning of their hostile relationship. And his motivation for helping Slocum was excellent: fear and self-interest. He watched the old woman prepare the salve her husband had brought from town.

"Well?" Eddie asked irritably. "What's next?"

"We sit here a day or two till I can move. In the meantime we find out what's on everyone's mind." He turned to the old man.

"What's your name, *señor?*" Slocum spoke pretty good Spanish.

"Sebastiano Valdes, *a sus órdenes.*"

"William Pearson," Slocum said, bowing from his prone position. "Eduardo Sheridan, Samuel Hannum." The two men nodded curtly. Slocum knew the importance of politeness with Mexicans, even if the other two did not. Politeness solved many problems south of the border.

"Eddie, will you get me my saddlebags?" Slocum asked. Eddie got them without complaining. He had taken them along from Saragoza. Slocum took out a twenty-dollar gold piece and gave it to Valdes. The old man held it with awe in his leathery, callused palm. No doubt it was the first one he had ever seen, let alone owned, Slocum was sure. He took out two more, showed them to old Valdes, and replaced them. "One for today," he said, "one more for each day we stay here—"

"Sixty bucks so far!" Sam said, aggrieved. "That's as much as I get in a month!"

"He's gonna *earn* his," Slocum said. Eddie tittered.

Slocum said he would pay Valdes well for accurate information on certain topics. If the information he received was not correct, he, unlike the general, did not have to cross any rivers to show his disappointment. Old Valdes sat with his gnarled hands in his lap. He nodded calmly. Slocum began writing something as he spoke to the old man.

"First," Slocum began, "where is Watts? Second, when I was a guest of the general's I heard someone talk about a federal army on its way up from Chihuahua to deal with him. Where is this army? And the third. You will give this note to the general—"

Valdes shrugged, smiling.

"What's the matter?"

"The general cannot read. He will have to give it to someone to read for him. There will be a priest, maybe—he will not trust the priest. So—" Valdes shrugged again.

Slocum tore up the note.

"But he knows me. I will tell him."

Slocum told Valdes what he wanted the general to know. The old man rose, said "I'm going," and disappeared.

"What you gonna do now?" Sam asked nervously.

"You're gonna get the old lady all the water and firewood she wants. Then you're gonna sit on that hill with Eddie an' fire a couple warning shots at anyone who gets too close."

"Yeah, but what you gonna do?"

"Sleep," Slocum said. "Just sleep."

At nine that night Valdes stepped behind Eddie on the ridge and coughed politely. Eddie hurled himself sideways in desperate haste and worked the lever of his carbine as he skinned the left side of his face on the rough ground.

"Soy yo!" shouted the old man. *"Amigo, amigo!"*

"God damn it!" Eddie got up and held his scratched face. "Y' almost got kilt, sneakin' up on me like that."

The old man did not speak English, but he knew what the translation would have been. He did not bother to explain that very frequently he did not approach his house by the trail. Ambush was too easy along the border. There were too many enemies. He simply came over the ridge, saw Eddie, and decided to cough as a well-bred way of attracting attention, to prove his intentions were friendly.

Valdes's wife shook Slocum awake. He felt much better. He could sit up without too much pain. He sat on the old shuck mattress with his back against the cool adobe bricks and lit a cigarette. The old man rolled one for himself and squatted. Sam leaned against the wall and watched.

"Were you followed?"

"No."

"Good. And Watts?"

"Señor Watts looked for your wagon toward Señor Sheridan's *rancho* for fifty miles. He then came back to Nacozari and sent a telegram to Señor Sheridan. It said you were dead, that your two men had refused his offer of help, and that unless he sent the wagon back with someone more intelligent the whole arrangement would be useless."

"How—" began Slocum.

But Valdes was shrewd and knew what the question would be. He answered it succinctly. "My niece's husband's son Emiliano sweeps the telegraph office. He has trained himself to read Morse. No one knows this."

"Very good. Next?"

"I went to Saragoza to sell some peppers at the

market. My cousin Hilario works there in the only hotel. He—"

In Mexico it was usually the women who went to market to sell. Slocum asked, "What did people say when you began to sell the peppers instead of your wife?"

"I said she had a sickness, but would be well in a few days."

"Go on," Slocum said. He liked Valdes.

"My cousin Hilario listens to everyone's talk. The army is marching from Chihuahua. They have artillery. They have many good officers, trained in *Francia*. They will have maybe five thousand men. Another army is coming from Monterrey. They will squeeze the general between them; that is the plan. It is said they have orders to take no prisoners."

Slocum grinned. "And the third?"

"The general will meet you where you say."

"Muchas gracias."

"Por nada, señor. It is nothing."

"What's he say?" Sam asked.

"Tomorrow at noon," Slocum said, looking at the ceiling and smiling in anticipation, "I meet the son of a bitch at Isla Culebra."

"Oh, shit," Eddie said morosely. "*Snake* Island. Where is it?"

"It's an island smack in the middle of the Rio Cuajaran. It's not the States and it's not Mexico. It's neutral."

"You don't look neutral."

"I don't feel neutral." Slocum replied.

"What I can't figger out is why this ol' guy's riskin' his life helpin' us. Jus' fer the money? The gold's real good pay, but it ain't enough. What's in it fer him?"

Eddie suspected everyone. He went on, "I know they took his goats an' I know they shot his nephew. Still . . ."

"Here's how they shot his nephew," Slocum said. "He had a burro loaded with two boxes. He told the general it was bread. The general asked him to sell him a little. The nephew said he could not because he was taking it to the owners of the Hacienda Santa Rosario. The general said, 'Sell us the bread or I will take it from you.'

"The nephew answered, 'In my affairs only I command.'

"The general shot him twice and killed him." Slocum fell silent.

"Yeah," Eddie said, after a few seconds, "that would do it."

Slocum continued. "We have a problem on this island. The general's going to want those carbines for nothing. He needs them very, *very* bad. He doesn't give a damn how he gets 'em or who he hurts gettin' them. We will have to be very neutral and very smart tomorrow."

"How many men does he have?"

Slocum asked Valdes. The old man looked up from his cold tortillas. "Maybe a thousand, maybe twelve hundred," he said.

"Is he goin' to bring 'em all to the island?" Sam asked.

"Not enough room. I know the island. It's very small. He'll have to leave the men and cattle back in Mexico and come alone to the island. I'll leave my army back in Arizona and go alone to meet him. He has his men bring over, say, thirty head from Mexico. I give him one carbine for them and a hundred rounds. He brings over another thirty head. I give him another carbine and a hundred more rounds. That way I don't get burned bad if something goes wrong, and he doesn't either.''

''It don't sound so good to me,'' Sam said.

Slocum lifted an eyebrow. ''You have a better idea?''

Sam chewed on a tortilla for a moment. ''What I don' see,'' he said slowly and painfully, ''is how we're gonna persuade this real rough *hombre* the three of us is an army. He's got an *army* out there, for crissake! When he sees there's jus' three of us with all those nice new Winchesters sittin' in crates like birthday presents, what's gonna stop 'im from rushin' us an' eatin' us alive? That dotted line in the middle of the river? I don' like it. No, sirree, I don't. I don' see why I gotta put my neck in no rope.''

''I agree,'' said Slocum. Sam looked surprised, then pleased.

Slocum went on, ''No reason for him not to take all the stuff and not pay for them. He's got a good reason to try and grab 'em. If he don't get 'em, he's dead. He doesn't care if he makes George Sheridan good and mad. But there's one good reason why he won't make that rush.''

''You're sure, Pearson? I ain't.''

''I am. We got an army.''

''You got fever, boy.''

''The old man and his two nephews and his two grandsons are gonna herd the stock and hold it for us once they're across the Cuajaran. You two are gonna look like an army.''

''Looky here, Pearson! I don't hafta go along with you that far. Not if you're that loco. I jus' wanna tell you—''

''We'll leave at sunup. We got lots to do before the general arrives on his side of the Cuajaran.''

"Yeah, but—"

"Hasta la mañana. I need sleep." Slocum turned over and pulled up his blanket. Sam stood up, looked at Valdes, rotated his forefinger in the air over his right ear several times, and pointed at Slocum.

The old man smiled and slowly moved his forefinger back and forth in the negative sign of Mexico.

"Oh, no, señor," he said. "Oh, no."

16

Isla Culebra was a low sandbar six hundred and fifty feet long. At its widest it was two hundred feet. It tapered to a sandy spit at both ends. On its upstream end driftwood had piled up into a tangle of branches. They were bleached white by the furious sun till they were the color of old bones. Low-growing shrubs grew in scattered clumps over the island. The Mexican side had a wide mud shoreline, cracked into flat slabs by the sun. Back of the shore, ocotillo and willow and cottonwood flourished so thickly that hundreds of men could hide in it totally unobserved from the Arizona side. The same impenetrability was true of the other shore; a hundred feet back from the shore was a small hill covered with dense shrubbery all the way to its crest.

Just after sunrise the wagon with its load of carbines and ammunition creaked to a halt. Valdes and his nephews and grandsons reined in. Slocum ordered Eddie and Sam to break open three cases. They were puzzled, but they obeyed orders; Slocum had not yet told them his strategy. As they pried open the cases he slowly and painfully got down from his seat on the wagon. Valdes dragged Slocum's saddle from the back of the wagon and saddled his horse.

Grimacing with pain, Slocum mounted.

The crates were open.

"All right," Slocum said. "There's thirty carbines in there. Load 'em."

Still puzzled, Eddie and Sam loaded.

Slocum turned to Valdes. He told the old man to scout the other side of the Cuajaran, see if anyone was there watching, and come back as soon as he made sure. He was to keep his men scouting the area.

The old man nodded and took his men across the river.

Slocum turned to the Americans. "You two spread out and scatter the guns behind bushes, in the forks of trees, anywhere it looks like a natural place to cover me when I'm on the island. Point 'em all toward me. If I move a little, move a couple of 'em, as if I'm still being covered wherever I go. When that's done, Eddie, you go on up the hill with your Springfield. Find a good place up there. Take plenty of water an' a bite to eat. Make yourself plenty of shade. You're not going to leave that place. You're not going to *move*, maybe till late in the afternoon. I want to be covered all that time. *Every second*. Or I'll tell your cousin George." He paused and looked at Eddie's face.

"Like the idea of me being in your sights?"

Eddie did not respond, but it was obvious to Slocum that he liked the idea very much indeed.

"You're pretty good with a rifle, George Sheridan says. Show me."

"Show you what, fer crissake?"

Slocum pulled a silver dollar from his pocket. "When you see this silver dollar held straight up in the air, I want it knocked spinnin'."

"Want the edge nicked, or want it hit dead center?"

"You serious?"

"Goddamn right I am, Pearson."

Slocum liked Eddie's calm assurance.

Eddie took his Springfield from under the wagon seat. "How 'bout a little bet?" he asked.

"All right. Ten bucks says you won't hit it dead center."

"You got a bet, Pearson."

"You're going to have to watch me real close all the time I'm there talkin'. And not take your eyes off me for a second."

"I'll watch you like you was a rabbit an' I was a hungry rattler."

"I'll bet," Slocum said dryly. "First thing, you and Sam set up the carbines till they look good to me."

"To the general too, huh?"

"To the general, especially."

Slocum rode into the water. The river came up to his stirrups. On the island Valdes rode out of the thicket and reported that no one had been there the night before and that there certainly was no one there now. Slocum told him to keep scouting.

"*Sí.*" Valdes nodded. "There's rattlesnakes there," he said, grinning, and rode off.

In an hour the carbines were properly set up. It looked as if a couple hundred men were covering every square inch of the island. The silence made them eerily impressive.

Three times, as Slocum walked back and forth correcting the angles of the carbines, he was challenged by big diamondbacks. The island produced fat rabbits, which explained the rattlers' presence. The heavy, massive brown diamond patterns blended very well into the fallen leaves and the broken shadows. But Slocum deliberately made noise as he walked. The rattlers flowed out of the way after the warning rattle. The rattles protruding vertically from the thick coils moved so fast they became dark brown blurs. Unlike many others in the West, Slocum did not automatically hate the snakes. He respected them because they usually gave warning, and they did not go out of their way to attack.

Quite unlike the general. Slocum smiled to himself at the thought. He called Sam over to the island.

"Looks good," Slocum observed. "When they get here, you and Valdes move from one gun to another. Sort of move the muzzles a bit, as if someone is covering me *every* time I move. Move 'em whenever the general or one of his men moves around. Once in a while, let 'em see a shirt or a hat. Cover a lot of ground. Move one of 'em far to the right, then one in the middle. One near the right again, then back to the left. You get it?"

"I gotta hand it to you, Slocum," Sam said grudgingly. He rode back to Arizona while Slocum sat in the shade of his horse drawing brands in the sand with a dried twig. The sun was about to touch the zenith when Valdes trotted into the river followed by his relatives. The young men were looking over their shoulders in an excited manner.

"They're almost here," shouted Valdes. "Many, many!"

Slocum told them not to act surprised if a shot should come from the hill above them. They should behave as if such shooting were common. They were to appear confident and serene, as if they knew that hundreds of men were backing them up.

"Think you can do it?" Slocum asked.

"We will do it," promised Valdes grimly. "I brought them up to show respect to a man who deserves it." He turned to the young men and asked, "Do you under-

stand what the *patrón* says?" They nodded. "Good,"
the old man said. "Is anyone scared?" No one spoke.
"Good," he said. "We are ready."

Almost immediately afterward the general appeared
on the shore. Several men followed him out of the
chaparral and spread out on either side. They carefully
scanned the other shore of the Cuajaran. But the general
was the first one to catch sight of the carbine muzzles
sticking out of the dense shrubbery. He turned and
spoke sharply. Two men trotted to the rear and disappeared into the thicket.

Slocum stood up painfully. The general took off his
sombrero and bowed ironically. Slocum nodded. The
general replaced the sombrero, grinned, and spoke to
Pablo, who laughed, holding his palm over his ruined
mouth. The two men rode into the river.

They looked down at Slocum while he began to
unstrap his bedroll from the cantle.

"Not nice, *amigo*," said the general reprovingly as
he jerked his head to the muzzles.

"I learn as I go along," Slocum said. He patted the
blanket beside him.

"No, no. I don't like it." The general still sat his
horse, frowning down at Slocum.

"You have me covered too. I'm not complaining.
Sit."

"All right, *gringo*," the general said with a sudden
grin. "I get off. We talk business." He dismounted and
gave the reins to Pablo. Up to now, Slocum had not
been able to get a good look at the man. Pablo had a
patch over one eye. Several of his front teeth were
gone. His nose was swollen to twice its normal size and
the area under his eyes was black and blue. Pablo took

the reins while he scowled down at Slocum, who calmly went on drawing cattle brands in the sand.

The general squatted on his haunches. "You are lookin' good," he said critically. "Well, mebbe not so good. But better than the last time I saw you, no?"

Slocum said nothing. The general picked up a twig and began drawing in the sand also. "You surprise me," he said. "I don' think you would get to Arizona. I don' think you live till mornin'. Funny," he went on, amused. "There is Arizona; back there is Mexico. One hundred feet, you kill me. One hundred feet, I kill you. Here we are, friends. Funny, no?"

"Funny," said Slocum. His green eyes glittered with contained rage.

"You make fun of me?" The general's voice was low with sudden tension, as if he were a coiled spring ready to burst. He was not used to people disagreeing with him.

"My back hurts, *amigo*," Slocum said. "I still don't see so good. You rub me a little too much the wrong way and I might just take you with me up shit creek. You know where that is?"

"I been livin' in Texas, *gringo*. I know the dirty way you talk."

"Suppose we get down to business right away. It's hot here, and I'm gettin' real thirsty."

The general said nothing for half a minute. His face was hidden under his sombrero rim as he stared at the ground and the patterns he was making with his twig. "You lucky," he said finally. "You lucky you got all those men there, Pearson," he went on, jerking his head at the carbine muzzles he could see poking out of the brush. "All right, we talk business. One more question I wanna ask you."

"Go ahead."

"How you feel when you get to the States?"

"Wet clothes in Arizona are a damn sight more comfortable than dry ones in Mexico."

"Hey, that's good!" shouted the general, in a swift change of mood. *"Oye, Pablito, ven acá!"*

Pablo shambled over, staring down with hatred at Slocum. The general translated Slocum's remark. Pablo was silent.

"Trouble with Pablo," said the general impatiently, turning back to Slocum, "is that ever since he lost his eye he thinks nothin' is funny. He—"

Pablo tugged the general's sleeve and whispered in his ear. The general's look of irritation vanished. A thoughtful look swept across his face. He turned to Slocum.

"Pablo thinks somethin' very funny," he said. "He thinks mebbe you don' have so many men there." Slocum looked at Pablo with an amused expression.

Pablo was staring at him closely.

"Porqué?" Slocum asked idly.

"Where would you get so many men so soon?" Pablo asked in Spanish, and shrugged.

"You think I'm bluffing?"

Pablo shrugged again, more elaborately. He smiled, covering his broken teeth with a large, dirty hand. Slocum took a silver dollar. Now was the time for a spectacular action which, if carried out perfectly, would end all doubt. He handed it to Pablo.

The man stared at it in bewilderment.

"It's yours, *amigo*," Slocum said. "It is a magic dollar. Very heavy. I bet you can't hold it straight up in the air for five seconds."

Pablo stared at him suspiciously.

"Afraid?" Slocum asked.

Pablo thrust his arm high, staring at Slocum. Slocum smiled with a confident air, but inside he was praying that his trust in Eddie's marksmanship would be justified.

Four seconds later the dollar leaped out of Pablo's hand as if it were alive and spun away in a silver blur. While it was still spinning there came the harsh crash of the Springfield's explosion. The general snapped his head around and stared at the hill. A tiny puff of smoke drifted away. He bent down and picked up the dollar. The hole was dead center. The general looked again toward the Arizona shore. Two carbine muzzles shifted a little. It was clear that each movement of the general was being faithfully reflected in gun movement. There was the flash of a blue shirt behind a tree fork.

"Hey, *gringo,*" the general said thoughtfully, "you wanna work for me? I pay good. Money, women, all you wan'." He looked again at the hole in the dollar.

"Bring him, too," he added as he pointed to the hill.

Slocum shook his head.

"We have a good time," the general went on. "We drink plenty *pulque*, mebbe for you we get weesky, we take plenty of *Nañita's* cattle—"

"Whose?"

"*Nañita, nañita!* Grandmother. That's what we call all the cattle in Arizona. You don' know this word? No? You gringos stole Arizona, no? All that cattle over there—" he waved his hand casually all along the Arizona shore—"all that cattle over there is *Nañita's*. We jus' come once in a while an' take it back. Well, we sell them to rich *hacendados* in Sonora, Nuevo León. Nobody very particular down there 'bout 'merican brands. Or mebbe we go sell 'em in Texas. Nobody care too much exceptin' Cattlemen's Association inspectors, but how many men they got? So. We take the money, we put it in a bank in Francia, Italia. Three, four years from now we go to Paris, eh? We be *very* rich, *gringo!* You plenny smart; you got *cojones*. Why we fight? Pablo ain't so smart an' he ain't good no more. I gotta get rid from him.''

''No.''

''I make you a general too, like me.''

''No.''

''You like that girl I got, Luisa de Parral?''

Slocum felt his heart jump, but he kept his face without expression.

''You come with me, you can have her.''

Slocum felt his heart jump again, like a trout after a fly. He thought that all this talk was a very well thought-out trap. He would have to watch his way here carefully. He shook his head slightly.

''No? I thought you like this one. Nobody touch her yet. Mebbe me, a little.'' He cupped his hands at his chest. ''She nice here.'' He grinned. ''Oh, she fight, she fight!''

''No,'' Slocum said. The thought of this animal with the de Parral woman sent waves of hatred through him. But he had a very good card to play. He could wait.

''You wan' to get to business? You *norteamericanos*, all the time business, business! All right. You see. We start. First thing, I give good stock, no culls. You send one carbine, one hundred cartridges across to Mexico, I send across twenty head. You—''

''Twenty-five.''

There was silence. The general took several deep breaths before responding. Slocum had the ability to surprise him, and this particular move of his was totally unexpected. The general was displeased with himself for not expecting any more startling moves from this very clever *gringo*.

"Pearson, I make arrangements with Sheridan before I even know you, my fren'. Twenty—"

"Twenty-five."

The general looked down at the sand. He drew a circle with his twig and stabbed the little piece of wood deep down into the center of the circle. Slocum knew that the general was wishing that it was Slocum's heart at the end of the wood.

Without looking up he said slowly, "I don' like it much."

"Me neither, *amigo*. Twenty-five."

"No good to get mad. Me or you. Too hot. Too many pipple 'round here with guns, no? *Twenty*."

"Twenty-five," Slocum said. He was enjoying the general's attempt to control his obvious fury.

The general stood up. "You make jokes, *amigo*." He set a foot in his stirrup. "This heat makes you *loco*. If I don' take your guns, all you got is scrap iron. You goin' be in much trobble with Sheridan. Believe me."

Slocum grinned. "You gotta come back to me, and you know it," he said softly.

"Why, *gringo*?" The general swung a greasy trouser leg over the saddle and settled back.

"I bet you play poker pretty good," Slocum said. He was enjoying the game.

"Pretty good. Mebbe we play later when you work for me."

"We're playin' right now. You're bluffin', an' I got all the cards. *All* of 'em. Sit down."

"I don' like this talk. Say what you mean!"

"Listen good, *amigo*. In three days, maybe four, you're goin' to be fighting the Mexican army. They're

like you—no prisoners. You're not goin' to do too
well. Each man of yours who's got a carbine—and
that's only one out of four—has got only three or four
rounds left.''

"You keep your ears open, eh?"

"And I keep 'em washed. Not like you.''

The general flushed red. Slocum watched him, smiling.

Finally the general managed to get himself under
control.

"All right," he said thickly. "*Verdad*. I need them
bad. I give twenty-five."

"Not any more, *amigo*."

"What you mean? Mebbe I don' onnerstan' you
English. Mebbe—''

"You understand all right. You might have dirty
ears, but you hear just fine. Since we've been arguin'
about price I've been gettin' thirsty. And every time I
get thirsty the price goes up. So now we stand at
thirty.''

Sweat dripped off the end of the general's nose. He
stank like a horse after a hard day's work on the range.
His eyes glittered with hatred. When Slocum thought of
those big, filthy hands cupping Luisa de Parral's breasts
it was all he could do to refrain from jerking the
general from his horse and kicking him. The general's
hands were twisting the reins so tightly that his knuckles had turned white. Finally he spoke.

"Some day we meet again, *gringo*. Mebbe in hell. It
don't matter. I wait for you there, eh?''

"I had a day and a night to think about you, *general*.
You're gettin' off easy. Real easy. If I was really mad
I'd bust those carbines right in front of you and watch
you go crazy. To hell with Sheridan. But I'm nice.
Because I'm nice I'm gonna let you fight that federal

army with guns and ammunition instead of watching you get your ass shot off.''

"All ri'. I don' wanna talk no more. Thirty head, one carbine, one hundred rounds.''

"Two more things I want.''

It was only with great effort that the Mexican kept his face under control. He looked at Slocum with a heavy-lidded stare. It reminded Slocum of the unwavering, unblinking gaze of a rattlesnake.

Then he said slowly, "Well?''

"I want my horse back.''

"All ri'.''

"A good saddle to replace the one you ruined.''

"All ri'. How's your back, *amigo*?''

Slocum ignored that remark. He could afford to, since he knew he would enjoy the impact of his next request.

"And I want Luisa de Parral.''

The general's response was surprising. He leaned back in his saddle and smiled. He turned and spoke quietly to Pablo. Pablo's mouth dropped in amazement. He looked incredulous. The general repeated his orders. Pablo grinned, stared at Slocum, then rode into the river. The general turned to Slocum and said, "*Amigo*, if I don' have an army to fight ri' now, you know what I gonna do?''

"Sure. You'd finish where you left off with that branding iron.''

"Damn ri'.''

"If I didn't have you right in my sniper's sights. You forget that.''

"Hey, listen, *gringo*, no joke, you come with me. I make you a general, jus' like me. I don' lie. You bring your man with you, the one who shoot so good.''

Slocum grinned and stood up. He faced the Arizona shore and yelled, "One case carbines, one case ammo!"

Valdes and one of his nephews brought them to the island. The general disregarded Valdes's hard stare. Valdes had a small crowbar. He pried one case open. The general smiled as he took out the top carbine. It was heavily smeared with grease. He wiped his hands carelessly on his trousers. He worked the lever action lovingly, set the gun down, and wiped his hands once more on his trousers. He held up both hands as he faced the Mexican shore. His fingers outstretched, he closed both hands. He repeated this gesture three times. Several men on horseback nodded and rode away. Five minutes later they came out again with thirty head. Yelling and lashing with their doubled-up riatas, they forced the cattle into the water and toward Arizona. As they passed the island, Slocum scrutinized them carefully and rejected two.

The general made no objection. He whistled sharply and held up two fingers. Two more cattle were driven into the river. Valdes's nephews and grandsons met the cattle in the middle and swam them across.

The general said, staring at the Valdes men, "I think I know where you get your information, *amigo*." Slocum did not answer.

He sat on his blanket and looked at the little herd now being held on the Arizona side. George Sheridan had told him to ask for twenty head for each carbine. By the time Sheridan would get those cattle to railhead he'd get forty dollars apiece for them. That made eight hundred dollars per carbine. The cost of taking a lot of cattle to railhead would be very little when broken down per cow. Sheridan must have paid about fifty dollars per carbine. That was a damn nice profit, Slocum thought, and only a little risk was involved—all of which he, Slocum, was taking.

Slocum was getting thirty cattle per carbine. The extra ten were his. Sheridan hadn't planned it that way, of course. If the rest of the trading went well, and he could find a buyer, he would be doing very nicely. He knew very well he might have trouble with Sheridan about the extra ten he had swindled for himself. There might be some intense discussion about whom they belonged to. Slocum would risk that. He would have trouble with lots of people about those cattle—the Cattlemen's Association inspectors would want to know how he had possession of so many stolen brands. He would have trouble with Mr. Watts, with Comanches or Apaches who considered a tax on passing cattle logical since the white ranchers had driven off the buffalo and deer. There would be ranchers who would object to his cattle drinking their water, or who feared that his cattle might be carrying the Texas tick. He ran the risk of stampedes caused by so trivial a thing as a saddle slicker crackling on a rainy night as a rider turned in the saddle. An hour's run would burn ten pounds off each animal—and, translated into so much per pound, that could run into plenty of money. But all those were risks he was willing to take.

The afternoon wore on to the quick dusk of the border river, and the Mexicans withdrew. Slocum splashed across to the Arizona side. After a restless, wary night in which everyone took turns standing guard with the cattle and waiting for a possible attack by the general, he rode again to the island after a quick breakfast of tortillas, beans, and black coffee, and began again the job of counting and exchanging.

By the time Luisa appeared on his horse on the southern shore, most of the cattle had been crossed. Both of her hands rested on the pommel of the saddle the general was giving to Slocum as part of the deal. Pablo led the horse by its reins. She rode astride. When the horse waded up out of the river the water cascaded down her long legs. Slocum looked at them and felt a warmth stir in his groin. It had been a long time since he had slept with a woman, and this woman had a simmering sensual appeal he found exciting.

Her right cheek had a large purple splotch. Pablo's face had also acquired several fresh scratches. They were still bleeding. He noticed Slocum's curious, icy stare. He grinned and wiped the blood away with his sleeve. She had now come close enough for Slocum to see that her wrists had been tied to the pommel.

"She don' wan' to come, *gringo*," the general said lazily. "Mebbe she don' like you. Pablo, would the lady prefer to stay with us?"

Pablo giggled, hiding his mouth.

"Yes, yes, she didn't want to come here!"

Slocum reached out and cut her loose. She rubbed her wrists while she stared at Pablo and the general. She looked at the boxes of carbines being opened.

"Am I being traded for guns?" she asked in perfect English.

"Not exactly," Slocum said. "You are a sort of condition for the sale; put it that way."

"Are you helping this—this *animal*—to fight against Mexico?"

At the word "animal" the general flushed. Slocum thought that a man with some sort of revolutionary movement fighting against centuries-old oppression might be said to be fighting *for* Mexico, no matter how bandit-ridden he was, but he knew that this was no time to get into a discussion.

The general's hand went to his quirt, but Pablo's warning touch on his elbow stopped him. He swerved his glance and saw that Slocum's right hand was resting lightly on the butt of his Colt.

The general turned his back on her and asked, "You got all the cattle now?"

"I got what I want. No reason for you to stick around any more. It's time for me to go north and for you to go south."

"Yes," said the general slowly. "An' we meet again some day, eh? The road is long, they say, but narrow enough, so we meet once more. I will like that." He turned his horse's head without a backward glance, but Luisa suddenly spoke.

"*Momentito, mi general,*" she said. Her voice was filled with contempt as she said the title.

He deliberately kept his back turned to her.

In her perfect Spanish, she said, "The reason why people like you have been beaten by we Parrals, and why your women were taken by the men of my family—"

Slocum did not think this was a generous thing for her to say. There was too much bitterness in the truth of it all. Her voice was filled with cold loathing. She went on.

"—is because you are vermin."

She had not raised her voice. The general jerked his reins hard and stopped his horse. His face showed all the hatred that his people had felt for centuries of arrogant Spanish domination. She continued. "Since you are animals you must be treated like pigs, snakes. Some day, *puerco*, I will put my heel at your throat and kill you."

The general stared at her. His face twitched. "Good-bye, you whore," he said, and spat into the river. He turned his horse once more to face Mexico. She reached quickly before Slocum could stop her and pulled his Colt from its holster. She had the hammer back before Slocum knocked her arms upward. The blast burned his face and the bullet screamed harmlessly. Before she could fire a second time Slocum wrestled the gun away, but in that moment the general had spun around and lashed at her face with his quirt.

Slocum carefully and quickly hit the general on his face in exactly the same place with the barrel of the Colt. It laid the flesh open to the bone. Then he jammed the muzzle three inches deep into the man's stomach. The general doubled over in agony. His bleeding face touched the pommel. Slocum covered Pablo with the gun. Pablo's hand had gone for his machete and had lifted it high in preparation for the deadly downstroke, but a bullet from Eddie's Springfield smashed his wrist.

He screamed, dropped the machete, and clasped the broken jumble of splintered bones with his left hand.

"*Muy buenas tardes,*" Slocum said dryly. He waved them into the river with his Colt. The general pulled himself erect. He held onto the pommel, which by now was slippery with his blood.

"Oh, I see you again some day, *gringo,*" he gasped. "Wait. Her too."

Slocum didn't doubt it.

He watched them cross the river, his Colt resting on his thigh. He was thinking: *That son of a bitch Eddie— now I have to be grateful to him.*

17

"What's he gonna do with them thirty extra carbines we got left over?" demanded Eddie. Sam and Eddie were sitting at the small campfire. In back of them was the low, squat mass of the Valdes house. The moon had risen and the wind had sprung up. Eddie was cleaning his beloved Springfield.

"Aw, don' talk so loud," Sam said. "He'll hear you."

Eddie looked over his shoulder at the Valdes house. "Yap, yap, yap, like an ol' squaw," he said sarcastically, but he lowered his voice. "How we gonna take back five thousand head? We need fifteen good hands fer that. Where we gonna git 'em? Take three weeks to make the ranch. I don' aim to swaller that much dust."

"If it takes three weeks, it takes three weeks, you pipsqueak. You'll swaller dust like the rest of us. Oughta put a bridle on your fat mouth."

Eddie went on as if he had not heard. "An' the *woman*," he said. "Woman on a trail drive—never heard o' such a thing. Didja?"

Sam scraped up the last of the beans from his tin plate. He looked at Eddie, swallowed, and wiped his mouth with his sleeve. He said, "Y' never trailed a herd nowheres, you punk kid. All y' ever did was hang 'round a saloon 'n' try to git some gal in a fam'ly way, but they wouldn't let you come near 'em, pimple face.

Now shut up! You got first watch. I'm gonna sleep. Stay away from 'er. She'll claw your face to rags you stick it too close. She'll go over that ugly map o' yours like a mountain line goin' up a pine tree.''

He spread his tarpaulin, undid his blanket roll, and tucked himself in. His head was almost vertical against his saddle. He tilted his sombrero over his face to keep out the light from the fire, and he closed his eyes.

"He's saddlin'," Eddie suddenly said. "Where's he goin'?"

"Ask 'im," Sam said with an amused grunt.

Eddie said nothing. Slocum walked into the Valdes house. As he walked by Luisa's bed she said, "Señor Pearson."

"Yes?"

"You are leaving me alone?"

The two black braids hung down. She had bathed and was naked under the blanket while her dress was drying.

"I'll be back."

She was silent a moment. She leaned forward, holding the blanket tightly. One braid swung back and forth. She caught it and held it still. The movement of her arm brought one full, ripe breast into view. Again Slocum felt excitement.

"Pablo raped me this afternoon," she said. "When he came to take me to the island."

She stared at him. His heart began to thud so violently that he was sure she heard it, that Señora Valdes, curled up in her bed in the other corner with the tiny fire glittering on her gold earrings, had heard it too. But the old lady snored softly.

He realized that if he hadn't insisted on her delivery as part of the deal she probably would still be untouched; that in the wild, headlong preparation to escape from the federal army and its summary executions she could very well have been left behind as unimportant baggage.

"I'll see you get to New Orleans," Slocum said thickly. His face felt hot and his hands seemed enormous and clumsy. Rarely in his life had things gone so sour for Slocum, and he did not like the feeling. "From there you can get a ship to Vera Cruz. Then you—"

"My fiancé is in Mexico City. He will not want me now."

"But your hacienda?"

She shrugged.

"Where do you want to go?"

She shrugged again. She leaned back, sitting up straight. The position thrust out her breasts. "You take me with you. Now."

"Tomorrow."

"Not tonight?"

"I'm busy." He took out his Colt and gave it to her. "Know how to use it?"

She smiled with relief and nodded. "You come back?"

"Later."

"And you won't leave me alone here in Arizona?"

"No."

She smiled again and settled back.

Slocum rode into Nacozari. The saloon was half empty. Watts was nowhere in sight. Slocum's horse moved, his hooves muffled in the thick dust. Watts lived in a frame house, unusual for Mexico. The winters were too cold for such construction and the summers too hot, but Watts disliked adobe; he thought it was common.

Slocum dismounted. He pulled the Winchester from the saddle scabbard and sauntered down the street. Over his left arm he carried a small canvas sack. Through the half-drawn curtains he saw Watts sitting at a table under a strong kerosene light. He was eating a thick ham sandwich on white bread—something else that set him apart from the average Mexican—and he was making entries in a ledger. Behind him was the huge black mass of a locked safe. On the table, close to Watts's right hand, lay a Colt. Watts took a bite from the sandwich, made an entry in the ledger with a pen he kept dipping into an inkwell, then he drank some beer out of a glass. He had a smug expression that Slocum looked forward to wiping off very quickly.

Slocum tapped quietly at the window. Watts put down his half-eaten sandwich and grabbed the Colt. He unbolted the door and peered into the darkness. There were no such things as street lights in Mexican towns. *"Quién es?"* he demanded.

"A message from the general," Slocum said gruffly in Spanish. He held up a folded square of paper.

"Not so loud!" Watts said nervously. There were federal troops in the town. "Come in, come in!" He lowered the Colt and stepped back. Slocum went in. Watts bolted the door and held out his hand for the message as he was turning around.

He looked into the muzzle of the carbine Slocum held five inches from the end of Watts's nose. His face drained white.

"Very slow," Slocum said gently. "Very slow, now. Give me the Colt. No sudden moves."

Watts did as he was told. Slocum stepped quickly into a corner of the room so that he could not be seen from the street.

"Pull the curtains all the way."

Watts did so.

"Take a seat, Mr. Watts."

Watts went back and sat in his chair. He still held the glass of beer in his left hand. His knuckles were so white that Slocum thought the man might actually break the glass.

"Finish eating while I talk."

Watts picked up the sandwich and took a small bite, staring at Slocum in a kind of paralyzed dread. He was unable to swallow.

"Throat too dry, maybe," said Slocum. He sat down opposite Watts and rested the carbine in his lap. He had shoved Watts's Colt into his gun belt. "Drink some more beer," Slocum said.

As Watts's hand reached out Slocum said genially, "This thing is pointed straight at your belly. Don't get smart and throw the glass at me. Don't try to turn the table over. This carbine is cocked and it has a *very* light pull. If you don't believe me, just make a move I don't fancy."

"What do you want?" Watts asked hoarsely. There were a lot of gray hairs in the stubble of his unshaven face. He suddenly looked old and shrunken. Slocum felt a little bit sorry for the man.

"Aren't you going to welcome me back to Mexico?"

Watts sat silently. Sweat formed on his forehead. He wiped it away with the back of one hand. He swallowed. Slocum leaned forward and prodded his stomach with the muzzle.

"Welcome back," Watts said tonelessly.

"Much better," Slocum said. "After my visit down here, which I must admit you did your best to make interesting, I'm getting used to the Mexican habit of talking about the weather and the relatives before getting down to business. How's Mrs. Watts?"

No answer came. Slocum prodded him again.

Watts grunted as the muzzle dug into his pot belly. "Fine," he gasped.

"Your father?"

"Dead."

"Sorry to hear that. How's your sister?"

"Ain't got a sister."

"We sure could use some rain hereabouts, couldn't we?"

"Yeah."

"Good," Slocum said approvingly. "You're not exactly boiling over with gossip, but that's not a bad try. Now let's get down to business. I could kill you now and get away and no one could catch me. Or even know it was me that had done it. And you wouldn't blame me at all. Would you, Mr. Watts?"

Watts stared at him. His lips were as gray as the stubble on his chin, but when Slocum began to feel sorry for him again he thought of the long night he had spent with his arms twisted high in the air behind his back. Then he did not feel sorry at all.

"Look at my eyes, Mr. Watts. And tell me what you see."

Watts licked his lips, leaned forward and peered into Slocum's face. "They look sorta red," he said hesitantly.

"You know why?"

Watts shook his head.

"Your friend the general has a great sense of humor. I'm not in a very good mood. But we can still do business. I've got twenty-seven hundred head, two-year-olds, no scrubs. They're all yours at twenty bucks a head. A real bargain. You want to buy them, right?" He leaned forward and prodded Watts again with the muzzle.

Watts grunted with pain and nodded assent.

"Good. That's fifty-four thousand bucks. Also with 'em I'm offering thirty carbines. Winchesters. Never been fired, just had the grease wiped from them, and after a day's exercise we put 'em back in their crates, good as new. I'm offering those at a hundred apiece. That's a a real bargain, too."

"*One hundred!* I can get all I want for forty!"

"Yeah. I know. But this is a real special bargain."

"What's so special about it?"

Slocum looked at him with a hard glint in his green eyes. Watts felt himself flinching. Slocum leaned back carefully. His back still ached, and he sought to find a position which gave him the least pain. When he had found it he spoke.

"Special," he said patiently, with his teeth set hard, "because they're offered by me. Call it a bonus because of the welcome I got from your buddy, the general. Now, Mr. Watts, I feel like I've already wasted a lot of your time. It's getting late and all. You'll be wanting to get to bed. That'll be a grand total of fifty-seven thousand. Since you and I know you got it all in that safe there, just get it out. Thank you kindly."

Watts kneeled on the floor and turned the combination lock. For half a minute he spun it back and forth, the clicking of the tumblers making the only sound in the room. Finally he pulled the handle down, swung the big door out, reached in—and grabbed the loaded Colt placed inside on the top shelf for just such an emergency. He shielded himself behind the safe door, spun around, and lifted the Colt with a triumphant expression.

Slocum was not there. He had moved quietly around the back of the safe, and from his new position Slocum poked the carbine into Watts's back.

"And one makes two," Slocum said cheerfully. He reached out and took the Colt from Watts's hand. He shoved it into his belt.

"Spoils of war," he said. "Don't go around saying I stole 'em, either. Man pulls a gun on you, you got a right to take it. An' you can sell those cattle for a nice profit up north. Don't know why you take on so."

Watts began to count out the money.

"Sell 'em, hell," he snarled. "Them're George Sheridan's cattle, an' he'll grab 'em!"

"No, they're not Sheridan's cattle," Slocum said. "They're *my* cattle. Deal was twenty head per carbine. I saw my chance and got thirty. Of course, if it hadn't been for your kind help the deal would've gone through for twenty. You're sort of tied up in this whole arrangement, in a manner of speakin', Mr. Watts. George Sheridan is gettin' what he bargained for. You got a nice touch when you count out greenbacks, Mr. Watts," Slocum went on with admiration. He reached out for the money, stepped back, and counted it, with a wary eye on Watts. The man might very well have a derringer stashed somewhere. "Hope you don't mind my checkin' up on your count, Mr. Watts," he said with a grin.

Watts's color had come back as soon as he was sure Slocum had no intention of killing him. "It don't pay to get me mad at you, Pearson," he said as he watched Slocum sweep the money into the canvas sack he had brought with him. "It would be real smart if you just gave me back that money and rode away. We got long memories down here. Sooner or later—"

"Shut up. Sit down at the desk." Slocum's icy voice cut away at Watts's recently gained assurance.

"Get me one of your nice receipts."

Watts got it.

"If you had a derringer stashed away in that desk drawer," Slocum observed, "I would've let you shoot me. Just out of good manners. It wouldn't be decent to take three guns off you in one evenin'. Go on now. Write 'William Pearson, Esquire'—be sure, now, to put in that 'esquire'—'has sold me twenty seven hundred head of cattle, range delivery, at twenty dollars. Also he has sold me thirty new Winchesters, .44 carbine model, at one hundred dollars each.' Good. You don't have to write down the total. I understand it's too painful. Now write the date on top and put your John Hancock at the bottom. Now give it to me. No, not yet! Wave it around a bit and dry it. There, that's better, isn't it? Pick up your herd at the Valdes ranch. The carbines'll be there. Ride an' make the cow count with old Valdes. He's smart and he knows cattle. If the count isn't right, tell him. I'll make it good. Any questions?"

"The Valdes fam'ly been a great help to you, ain't they?"

Slocum stared at him. Watts dropped his eyes and coughed nervously.

"One more thing," Slocum said. "Almost forgot." He pulled a small, filthy, sweat-soaked piece of paper from a hip pocket. It had been soaked in the Rio Cuajaran at least once. He opened it carefully and held it up for Watts's inspection.

"Know it?"

"Looks like a piece o' my stationery."

"Yep. It's an order of yours for fifty rolls bobwire."

"I don't need no bobwire."

"Mebbe yes, mebbe no. But you wrote it out. So you owe me four hundred more bucks. Damn fair price." Watts stubbornly refused to move. Slocum waved his muzzle toward the safe in silence. Watts took another look at the green eyes, which were filled with hatred so intense they seemed to crackle. Watts sighed and opened the safe again.

Slocum counted the money. "If I ever come back this way," he said, as he put the money away, "don't start with me, Watts. I'm feelin' grateful to you just now because you put me in the way of this fifty-seven thousand. So we'll just let the matter of this treatment by your friend drop. But I'll always be mighty touchy where you're concerned. And I aim to be around these parts for a long time. Better lock up the safe. The money in there looks mighty tempting, friend."

"Lucky you're honest," growled Watts.

"*Vaya con Dios,*" said Slocum. He blew out the light on the table and closed the door behind him. He thought of Watts sitting in the room in darkness and grinned.

The moon had set. Somewhere in the dark town a dog was barking, over and over. He thought of Luisa asleep with her hand on the butt of his Colt. All the ride back to Rio Cuajaran he kept thinking of her long white legs opening to take him. But she had been raped; she had been a virgin until then. The chances were that she would find him repulsive, as she would find all men for a long time.

Great patience and tenderness were needed to deal with her, and he simply did not have the time.

He crossed the Rio Cuajaran without being ambushed.

The general was busy elsewhere, preoccupied with the federal troops. Slocum smiled as his horse climbed up the Arizona shore. At least he had given the Mexican bastard a chance to go on fighting. But he did not think the general would be grateful. The whole country was filled with ungrateful sons of bitches.

18

In one corner of the adobe house Luisa was sleeping. From somewhere Señora Valdes had produced an old faded blue cotton nightgown and had loaned it to Luisa. In awe at the fact that a daughter of the *Conquistadores* was a guest in her house, she had extracted the nightgown, presented it to Luisa, and withdrawn to let her high-born visitor sleep in privacy.

Slocum came in. The oak shutters were closed, and a single candle burned on the low, simply built oak table in a corner. She was asleep on her back. One arm was flung over her head in an unconscious imitation of a Spanish dancer; the other was bent at the elbow, with her palm resting on her flat stomach. The blue nightgown was buttoned primly up to the throat. He could see where her nipples strained against the thin fabric. His eyes moved down to her stomach, over where her hips flared against the taut cotton, and down the long thighs and calves to her slender brown ankles. When his eyes traveled up again to the tightly buttoned top he suddenly became aware of her amused stare.

He flushed. He did not know that it was the best thing he could have done at that time. No single act could have more effectively proven to her that this man would never rape anyone. It gave her confidence in his integrity.

She placed one palm on top of the other, like a

slender brown goddess. Her breathing quickened. He was unshaven and he stank of sweat. He was suddenly aware of this and he started to move away. She reached out and caught his right hand.

She unbuttoned her top buttons with her left hand. Slocum stared as she pulled out her right breast. She suddenly gripped him around his wrist and pulled him down beside her. Her grip was fierce. He was surprised to see how strong it was. Once he was beside her, she pulled the gown from her shoulders to her waist.

Slocum felt his penis swell against his pants with an intensity that was almost painful. She pulled his head down with both hands and pushed it hard against her breasts. As he sucked her nipples she gasped and made little whimpering cries.

Her hands reached his fly and unbuttoned it. She gasped as his big penis burst from the fabric's restraint. He pulled the gown over her head. Her breasts rose, firm, heavy as grapefruits, tipped with hard red nipples, as her arms went straight up in the air to permit the gown to slide off her body. He dropped the gown on the bed. He was kneeling now. She made him stand up as she pulled his pants down and off. Then she clasped him hard in her arms as she nuzzled his penis with her face. Her amazing, instinctive behavior was free and passionate. Her tongue darted out and made light, flicking touches against the length of his swollen and turgid shaft, on the blue veins that ran along the bottom of his penis. Then she ran her tongue around and around the tip of his penis till he felt he was going to burst. But she sensed it and, lowering her head, began to lick his balls while her hands ran up and down his back, feeling the big muscles; suddenly her whole hot, wet mouth took his penis inside and slid down till she almost choked.

Slocum could not stand it any more. He pushed her gently back on the bed. He knelt beside her and ran his tongue around her stomach, smelling her fragrant warmth. She moaned with pleasure. Around and around his tongue traveled, each circle widening until his tongue touched her pubic hair. She arched her back in anticipation and when his tongue reached the outer lips of her vagina she quivered. Up and down his tongue slid; she became so wet his whole face was moistened as he plunged his tongue deep inside her. She jerked and quivered like a restless mare; her breathing quickened, and when he let his tongue touch the swollen knob of her clitoris she exploded in a long, gasping moan. Then she shuddered again and again, each time with lessening intensity. Finally she quieted and lay inert, while her breathing paced back to normal.

It was not time to enter her yet, Slocum knew. She turned and kissed him; when he put his tongue in her mouth she pulled away, startled with surprise. But she bent her head forward a moment later and responded. She decided she liked it, and entered enthusiastically into the game. Once more he was aroused; this time he moved quickly. He pushed her onto her back, pulled her thighs apart, and kneeled between them. He put his penis inside and she moaned in pain.

"I am torn up inside," she said.

Slocum withdrew. He could have forced her, but that was not his way. He would have to wait until she was healed. It would not be easy for him. He lay on his back. She leaned over him and said, "Look at the *gringo*, moody as an old bear." Slocum grinned. He took her in his arms. He could wait.

19

"Good stock," grunted George Sheridan with approval. He and Slocum rode through the rest of the herd. "They put on weight comin' up, looks like."

"Yep." Slocum recognized the accolade of the experienced cow man. They rode up a grassy slope and halted under a live oak. It was hot and windless. Sheridan dismounted and squatted in the shade. Slocum followed. His back still pained him, and his face showed it. The skin across the base of his spine had not yet healed. Sheridan eyed his slow movements shrewdly but said nothing.

"Lookit them buggers eat!" he said. "They got that pasture clipped like a lawn. Move 'em north t'morrow. They put on weight comin' up! You sure know your business, Pearson."

"Thanks."

"Another hundred pounds on 'em an' we'll take 'em up to the railroad. Heard you had a rough time down in Mexico."

Slocum nodded.

In exactly the same mildly sympathetic tone Sheridan added, "An' they say you're a cow thief."

"They say the same thing about you, Mr. Sheridan."

Sheridan grinned. "You ain't afraid of me at all."

"No."

"Heard you paid off your mortgage yestiddy, in full."

"You heard right."

"Some people are sayin' you paid it off with my money, Pearson." Sheridan's voice expressed nothing more than intrigued curiosity.

"It all depends how a man looks at it."

"I look at it that mebbe they're right," Sheridan said lazily. He rose and mounted. "So don't you figger you owe me a polite thank you?"

Slocum rode silently beside him. After a moment he said, "No."

"How come?" asked the amused Sheridan. "If it wasn't for me you'd still be grubbin' 'round with a lousy herd of mebbe seventy, eighty scrubs, all built like jackrabbits, crawlin' with worm, bawlin' for water, each worth mebbe four bucks. How'd you be able to tie 'em with that forty-dollar market at Abilene? How'd you take 'em 'cross that dry country full of 'paches if you was gonna try an' sell 'em to the miners? You couldn't afford to hire no one to trail 'em anywhere. And that's the God's truth." He lit a cigar. "An' you know it."

He looked at Slocum and waited.

Slocum said, "I worked for you two days in Mexico. I figure that I get all that I can for myself once you get the twenty head you bargained for."

Sheridan smiled. "You think you're a hard man. Remember this: I don't travel like a colt no more, but if you think you'll hold the coffin handles for me, there ain't no chance of that. *I'll* be the one lettin' you down easy with my hat off."

"I'll remember that, Mr. Sheridan."

Sheridan shrugged. He looked at the end of his cigar. He took a long breath and took his sombrero off. He swept it around the horizon. The sweep took in the big corrals, the windmills, the cattle sprinkled over the richly grassed hills and valleys. "Big an' pretty!" he said. "But, hot damn, wouldn't it be fun to tear 'er down an' start all over again?"

"Put on your hat," Slocum said dryly. "You'll get sunstroke."

"If I ain't already got it, eh?" He put on his sombrero. "You're makin' me a lot of trouble, boy. This de Parral girl who's fixin' to throw her shoes under your bed—"

Slocum stiffened. He had decided the best thing to do with her would be to send her back to Mexico. Slocum was not the marrying kind, and she was no casual conquest.

"Lemme finish, boy!" Sheridan went on. "I don't want a woman hangin' 'round here unless she's hitched. She's got everyone bellerin' 'an pawin' dust. I seen Eddie hangin' 'round her, nervous as a drop of grease on a hot skillet. You ain't staked out a claim on 'er, an' everyone figgers he's got a right to service the lady. No offense meant. I don't want no shootin' startin' over her."

"I'll take her over to my place tomorrow. Didn't want to do it till I got it fixed up a bit."

"I hope she ain't crazy. Don't look at me thataways. She sits all day an' won't say a word."

"She's not crazy."

"She acts like some women I saw after Indians got finished with 'em."

"I tell you she's *not* crazy."

"I knocked at 'er door this mornin'. No answer. Wanted to find out did she sleep comfortable an' would like 'nother blanket. No answer. Knocked again, pushed the door open. She's sittin' in the rockin' chair with that Colt you gave 'er layin' in her lap. She jus' pointed that cannon at me, an' then at the door. I closed that door as soft as anyone could wish. I don't argue with someone with that look. I don' want that woman runnin' 'round here with that .45. Sooner or later Cousin Eddie is gonna want some fancy huggin', an' if she don' wanna be hugged that little jerk is gonna be very dead. If she was mine, I'd slap that gun outta her hand an' paddle her bottom. But then I'd have trouble with you. Jus' tellin' you so's you c'n handle it pussonal-like.''

"She'll be gone tomorrow."

"Also, watch yourself goin' to town. My fam'ly is goin' 'round pawin' up the ground somethin' fierce at the idea of you makin' yourself a heap o' money out of this last deal of mine. They figger it's Sheridan money."

"You figure it's Sheridan money?"

"We been through that. Let's say you earned it. Wish you hadn't been so hard on Watts. With them prices you put on those carbines he'll come squallin' to me. If I wanna do more business with him I'll jus' have to pay 'im back everythin' in the long run.'' He grinned. "But I don' mind. It's time someone rubbed his nose in the dirt. This de Parral woman, you thinkin' o' marryin' 'er?"

"No."

"You like 'er more'n you admit, Pearson. I c'n tell by the way you look at 'er. Bet you don' know much 'bout women."

Slocum knew Sheridan was right.

"She looks like the kind made for this country. My wife wasn't. She came from a respectable city fam'ly in New Orlins, but when the baby came she was all right."

They were riding by the old cemetery. Slocum noticed that Sheridan averted his face. Slocum was sure that Sheridan didn't want to open old wounds by seeing the gravestones of his wife and young son.

After they had ridden past he went on. "That de Parral gal looks strong. Can handle a gun. My wife wouldn't go near one. She looks like good stock. Prob'ly part Indian. With her for a dam, my stock might improve." Sheridan grinned at Slocum's growing irritation.

"You ain't goin' after the general?" Sheridan asked, looking at Slocum's hard profile.

"No."

"You ain't takin' up her dare."

"I'm not crazy."

"Mebbe not so crazy. You spread the right flavor honey an' he'll come buzzin' 'round. When he gets his feet all sticky—" Sheridan slapped his palm hard against his thigh—"Squuush!" His horse skittered sideways a bit at the sudden sound, but he brought it back easily.

"And then?"

"Wait a minute. You gotta get 'im out of Mexico. You ain't gonna make the Rio Cuajaran at a run two times in a row. You gotta get 'im alone. That'll be hard; he likely won't go alone nowheres. An' with that son of a bitch Pablo, *that's* a hard case. Eddie says he lost an eye an' broke a couple teeth on account of you."

"Yep." Slocum grinned at the memory.

"So he'll be layin' for you. Jesus, Pearson, you got everyone layin' for you 'cept me, I reckon. That don' mean much. I always disagreed with everyone anyhow. You gotta think up some way to get the general alone."

They halted and dismounted. Old Valdes came up and took their horses. Sheridan watched the old man take the horses to the corral and get their feed ready.

"Good man, that Valdes," he said lazily. "You trust 'im?"

"Why shouldn't I?" asked Slocum, surprised.

"Can't tell when he'll turn on you, that's why," Sheridan said. "Ain't that your experience with Mexicans?"

Slocum stared at Sheridan's face, trying to probe for a meaning out of the calmly smiling surface.

"This Valdes—he ain't some sort of a friend of the general?"

"Not likely," Slocum said.

"He ain't sorta reportin' back on your next move, is he?"

"Not unless he's a mighty good actor."

"Better be sure to keep your thinkin' a secret from him when you work out your spiderweb. You'll need a couple good men you c'n trust. A hundred dollars a piece is gonna look real good to some poor Mexicans. Even if they like the general, a hundred bucks in gold looks mighty good. An' if it all works out all right you'll wind up the biggest *hacendado* in Sonora. With your know-how in this business an' you speakin' Mex pretty good, you could be a big man down there. An' all you need is a good idea an' some luck."

Sheridan threw his cigar stub away.

"Don' appeal to you, huh?"

"It still don't appeal."

"All right. No more. Get the men an' move the general's cows to the north pasture. We'll start road-brandin' tomorra."

Sheridan watched Slocum ride away. He lit another cigar slowly, as he always did when he was thinking very hard. He thought his plan for dealing with the general was a very good one. He could punch no holes in it anywhere. As a matter of fact, it appealed to him so much that he was going to do it himself.

20

Late the next afternoon Sheridan lay in his hammock, relaxing after a day's hard riding. He had already killed a third of a bottle of bourbon while Slocum was still sipping his second drink.

"I admire a man's built hisself up as fast as you, Pearson," he said thickly. "Takes brains." He sat up and straddled the hammock. Then he got off, swinging a heavy leg, and shifted to a nearby chair. He poured himself another glassful.

"An' takes a sharp eye. Pour yourself another drink, boy!"

Slocum filled his glass and sipped.

"An' takes somethin' else. Eddie, c'mere!"

"Whaddya want?" Eddie asked in his usual surly tone.

"Don' mumble, boy. Get here fast."

Eddie slouched up and leaned against one of the oak beams. He picked away at a dirty fingernail.

"Sit down, boy."

Eddie sat.

"Now stand up."

Eddie stood, baffled and irritated.

"Sit down." Eddie glowered and sat.

Sheridan turned to Slocum.

"Stand up."

Slocum did not move.

"You heard me, boy. Stand up!''

Slocum sipped bourbon calmly.

"Why ain'tcha standin' when I say so?"

"You better stop drinkin' if you want to fight, Mr. Sheridan."

Eddie swallowed with excitement and backed out of the way.

Sheridan stood. He wavered, but he managed to steady himself by laying a hand against a beam.

"I'm standin'," he said slowly. "You got 'ny objection to standin' *now?*"

"Nope." Slocum put his glass down carefully and stood up. Sheridan moved his heavy shoulders under his shirt a few times to limber up. Then his right hand flashed to his gun butt.

Slocum's hand reached his own gun before Sheridan's fingers touched his.

"An' it takes one more thing," added Sheridan. "Takes guts." He took his hand off his butt and sagged back into his hammock. Eddie's face hardened with disappointment.

"Get us some more whiskey, boy," Sheridan said. "We're gonna have us a tea party."

"Yo're lookin' to get yoreself kilt, George," his uncle Asa said. "Hung over bad?"

Sheridan growled.

"That Pearson, he don't look like much, George," Asa went on relentlessly, disregarding Sheridan's headache. "He drinks, but he don't lose control. You do. An' once—that's all it takes—just once, yo're gonna push 'im too far, an' he's gonna git his in first. Mark my words."

"I ain't markin' your words. Get me some coffee."

"You kept gettin' more 'n' more drunk. You disremember?"

"I don' remember nothin', ol' man."

"Better watch yourself. Ev'ry half hour you'd race 'im to see whose hand'd touch whose gun butt first. He allus won. He don' look like no two-bit rancher. More like a gunman. Then the both of you'd have another drink 'n' try again. He drank a lot, too. He wasn't spillin' any under the table like a dance hall girl, neither. You mought like 'im 'n' all, but I bet some fine day he'll blow a hole through you big enough for a blind man to piss through. Wait 'n' see, George."

"If I watched myself," Sheridan said holding his head with his eyes closed, "I'd be a broken-down cowpuncher with stove-in ribs shovelin' horseshit in a liv'ry stable in town, like you'd be doin' right this minute if you wasn't my uncle. I ain't never watched myself. That's why you're livin' here, that's why Eddie's got a job here, an' that's why you bunch of lousy bastards is gonna inherit the biggest goddamn ranch around here. An' that's why I like that Pearson feller. He don' watch hisself neither. He puts all his chips down, an' then he rides that wheel all the way till it stops rollin'. Now get the hell outa here. My head's killin' me."

"I'm tellin' you, George, you better watch out. That feller ain't—"

"It's no never mind! I like a man who fights with ev'rythin' he's got. Las' night I ran Eddie ragged. He took it. An' he's got *nothin'* to lose! You think I got 'ny satisfaction outa makin' that pup do tricks? I got me a man now who does the hard things I need done—an' he don't cry on my shoulder. He's hard an' he's smart. I'm tellin' you, it's gettin' to be a real pleasure for me, tryin' to outsmart 'im. The exercise is good for me."

"I don' know what the hell you're blabbin' about, George. What I say is, better gun 'im down 'fore he gits too big fer his britches. He's after that Parral gal, an' you, you damn fool, you been thinkin' you'd like a piece of that, not to mention her hacienda down there! Crissake, how's it gonna look if you 'n' 'im tangle over a Mex gal? I got a mind to pull out some o' his tail feathers myself."

Asa had been a hard man when he was young.

"You jus' do that li'l thing," Sheridan said as he plunged his head into a bucket of cold water. He pulled out his dripping head and fumbled blindly for a towel. Asa angrily threw him one. Sheridan chuckled. "Yep, you jus' try it. You wouldn't live long enough to eject the used cartridge."

"When you go to Mexico," she said fiercely into his chest, "I will go with you."

They were lying pressed closely together. He was running his fingers along the inside of her thighs. He felt moisture as her body prepared to take him inside.

"I am all healed inside," she said. Her hand ran down to his groin and cupped his testicles. He had been patient all this time, and now she had recovered her assurance and confidence. It had been very hard for him to hold himself back, and now was the time.

When she was wet and panting with anticipation she opened her legs wide and raised them high. He inserted the swollen purple head of his cock and she gasped with pleasure. He entered a half inch at a time, to the rhythm of her pleasure-filled moans. When he had fully penetrated her and was on the verge of withdrawing to come in again—slowly and gradually increasing the speed and violence of his thrusts—she locked her thighs around the small of his back so tightly that Slocum couldn't move.

She whispered in his ear, with tenderness, "I want you to kill Pablo for me. Promise me that. *Now*."

He promised.

"*Palabra de honor?*" she demanded, running her palms up and down his back.

This was something Slocum did not deal out lightly. He hesitated, thought about Pablo and the general and the night he had spent as their guest.

"Word of honor," he said.

"Ah," she said, "*now* fuck me hard!"

21

Slocum ripped open the letter from Nacozari. He was standing in the post office. It was a long letter, and Slocum looked at the signature. *Watts!*

He leaned against the wall and began to read it. The postmaster, another of George Sheridan's numerous relatives, was staring at him with what Slocum had come to recognize as the "Sheridan look"—a blend of anger, hostility, and puzzlement. The letter did not seem to have been opened.

The letter began without salutation.

"No use trying to explain. I guessed wrong about you. What gives me the feeling I can trust you is that the cattle on the Valdes place were just as you had represented them—and maybe a bit better. You're a hard man in a bargain, but a fair one. You and I could make a lot of money if we worked together. I know the border country inside out. I have contacts everywhere, and I can raise capital to finance big operations. But I need someone I can trust. I have my eye on a mining operation which ought to produce so fast it will make ranching look like chicken feed. If we get on I'll let you in on that.

"The reason why I'm writing is that you're on the way up. If you can't beat 'em, join 'em, that's my motto. In a couple of years you'll have a big spread. George Sheridan is only good for a few more years and from what I can see his kin will run that Big S into the ground come one bad winter. I need a good man to funnel my cattle in. You have some good men in the Valdes boys. Come down and we'll talk. To show my good faith I'm letting you in on a good thing: the general is finished. He's camped down about thirty miles in the States. The Mex army climbed all over him like a tomcat over a sick puppy. My army contact says the general can stay in the States, but he can't make speeches, and if he don't give up his guns and horses and mules the U. S. Army will come up from San Antonio and arrest him and that whole army of his and deport them across the Cuajaran, where the Mex army is waiting.

"So he will have to sell the stuff. Which he doesn't know yet. And he'll sell, you can bet on that. He has about 900 horses, 500 carbines, not too much ammunition, 250 burros, and about 3500 cattle. You might have some trouble with the Cattlemen's Association inspectors as far as the cattle are concerned, but I can make some deal with the Mex army people to let the cattle across the river. It'll cost a few thousand pesos. We could trail them anywhere. No need to tell you what the cattle would be worth. I hear Comanches are paying up to $100 for carbines. The British are offering $100–$150 for burros for the Zulu War. I'll let you in for half, and when we clear this up I'll work on some really big things for the both of us.

"Bring some men you can trust. The general's men are prowling around sticking up ranches, so you better be careful. Hope to hear from you soon. The army will move against him in two weeks from above date. Keep this confidential. Sincerely, Pete Watts."

Slocum put the envelope in his pocket. He walked two doors down, entered the barbershop, and took a chair. As the barber covered his face with a hot towel he leaned back and began some hard thinking.

If it were a straight offer he could do very well.

Was it a trap?

It didn't read like one, with that reminder to bring a reliable escort along. If he did go down he would always travel with the Valdes clan. He would ship out the best cattle and the best horses. He would handle the carbine deal himself. That would be a delicate operation, and he preferred to handle it alone rather than entrust it to Watts. It was the kind of deal which produced the fastest and largest profit, and it was all in cash.

Perhaps, he thought as he felt the warm, steamy towel around his face, the carbines should go north immediately. Watts could handle the cattle. He would say goodbye, shake hands with Watts, leave openly with the carbines and his bodyguard, and then slip back alone—or with the Valdes men—to find the general and kill him. With luck he would get Pablo also.

Then he would take the cash from the operation and ride into Sonora with Luisa. He would avoid coming near the border until everything had simmered down. A year or two. He would refuse Watts's further offers of deals until then.

The first thing necessary would be to telegraph Watts that he would be coming. He would have to do it from another town; there were too many Sheridans interested in every move he made. Then he had to find a buyer for his ranch. It would not do to arouse George Sheridan's suspicions. He knew that he could not sell it from Sonora through a land agent's office hundreds of miles away in a town controlled by Sheridan.

The more Slocum thought about it, the more he liked it. Watts would perform, unknowingly, the important function of bringing Slocum and the general together. Slocum would make an excellent profit, eliminate the general, and become the owner of a vast hacienda far bigger than Sheridan's ranch. It would take place so far south that he need not concern himself about Sheridan's desire to avenge himself.

Yes, he thought with a rush of satisfaction, better to clear out of the damn country. He would always have to be careful about the Sheridans—they would never forgive him for killing the old man. Sooner or later he'd be bushwhacked. Maybe someone would fire a shot from the sagebrush as he rode out into the blazing sun from a dark canyon, or a shot would crash into a window at night as he was eating supper.

But that would be what would happen even with Sheridan's restraining hand upon them. What would happen if that hand were removed?

"How's that, Mr. Pearson?"

He looked at the mirror absentmindedly. "Fine, just fine," he said with a nod. He put on his jacket, paid the barber and stepped out. He had to wire Watts and withdraw his account from the bank.

"Sure he didn't see you?"

"Sure, Mr. Sheridan," the barber said. It was the next afternoon. Wheat, the barber, held on to a stirrup. His other hand held a razor. "His face was all covered with a towel, even his eyes."

"Sure he didn't hear you open the envelope? Or see you readin' it?"

"Nope," Wheat said with smug assurance. "There was some kids yellin' an' playin' outside, an' a lot of big teams was goin' by. I wouldn't'a looked at a man's

private mail 'cept that the letter was from Nacozari an'
I know you got big innarests down there. Else," he said
virtuously, "I wouldn't'a touched it."

"I'll take care of you." He started to trot away, then
turned back. He whistled sharply. Mr. Wheat scurried
out eagerly.

"Mr. Wheat?"

"Yes, Mr. Sheridan?"

Sheridan said softly, as he leaned down, "you are
not to talk 'bout that letter to *anyone*. Never. At no
time. If I hear that you have, I'll be back for a talk."
He reached down, took the arm holding the razor, bent
the palm inward, and lifted Wheat's paralyzed forearm
until it was at the height of its owner's jugular. Then he
moved the arm quickly from left to right.

"Unnerstan'?"

Mr. Wheat nodded nervously. Sheridan grinned down
at him and cantered out of town.

"You really surprise me, Pearson," Sheridan said.
"Wantin' to sell out."

Slocum shrugged. "Can't work for you an' run a
ranch at the same time."

"Hire someone. Someone you c'n trust." He leaned
forward out of the hammock and said, "Git yourself a
light from my cigar."

Slocum leaned forward and puffed. Their eyes met.
Slocum had the sudden feeling that Sheridan knew he
was lying, but he dismissed it as the workings of a
guilty mind. As Sheridan leaned back and stared at him
in a friendly fashion, Slocum was sure he was imagin-
ing things.

"Too hard to find anyone," he said casually. "And

any money I plow back into that ranch—artesian wells, windmills, bobwire, blooded stock—that's all wasted unless I can be there steady. An' the taxes eat away at my bank account.''

"It's hard to find a man you c'n trust.''

"So I figure, sell it for a good price, put the money into U. S. bonds, get a good, safe interest rate, no risk, work for you for a few years, bank that money, and then I can start off clean.''

"Fair 'nough. What're you askin'?''

"Stock, house, corrals, as is—eighty-five thousand.''

"That's a lot.'' Sheridan frowned.

"World couldn't beat it for a good summer range.''

"That's true. I'll go 'long with that.''

"And couldn't be beat neither for winters.''

Sheridan nodded. Slocum continued, "Plenty arroyos with willow and cottonwood. Good shelter from north winds. When it snows cattle can find their way there real easy. You could store fodder there. When snow melts, I got some clay tanks built at the bottom of the runoffs to catch the water and hold it all summer. Rollin' country there means cattle could climb some an' let the wind up there blow away the flies. Means more pounds at railhead.''

"You know your ranchin', all right. I'm glad you'll be givin' your full time to the Sheridan spread, Pearson. Gimme four years an' you ain't gonna want your own place. It's excitin' runnin' a place as big as this one. Lately I been thinkin' it would be real nice to unbuckle my gun belt an' throw it in the fire an' watch a smart bugger run it. Eighty thousand.''

"Eighty-four.''

"Eighty-one.''

They grinned.

"Eighty-two five."

"Done!"

They shook hands on it. "I'd like a week off," Slocum said casually.

"Sure."

"Want to go up to Flagstaff an' buy the bonds."

"What about your gal?"

"I'm takin' her along. She'll go on the train to San Francisco and then take a boat to Mexico. Safest way, with all those rebels shootin' up Sonora."

"Thought she didn't want to go back."

"Thought so too, but I talked her into it."

"All right," Sheridan said. He grinned and started the hammock swinging by shoving his boot at the floor. "I'll have the *dinero* tomorra afternoon." He laced his hands behind his neck and watched Slocum walk out.

"Eighty," Sheridan said, "eighty-one. Eighty-one five. Eighty-two. An' eighty-two five."

Slocum put the money into his saddlebags.

"I'd feel better if you counted it."

"I trust you," Slocum said. He gave the bags to Sebastiano Valdes, who took them outside. Through the doorway Sheridan watched as Valdes threw the saddlebags across Slocum's saddle.

"Well, now," Sheridan said lazily, "that's a real nice compliment. Mighty nice." He noted that Sebastiano's nephews rode good horses and were well armed. Two burros carried their food and bedding. Luisa sat waiting. Sheridan stood up and walked outside with Slocum. "Take care of yourself," he said cheerfully.

"I don' wanna lose a good man. *Adiós, señorita, vaya con Dios.*"

"*Y usted. Gracias.*"

"*Hasta la vista,* Pearson."

"*Hasta la vista.*"

He watched them ride off.

Sam Hannum came out and said, "You're crazy! Givin' him all that money! You know he's got a lot more on 'im? Why won't'cha let us bushwhack 'im? We could ride ahead an' pick 'em off tomorra at sundown. They gotta make camp in Arroyo Hondo. With Eddie an' me an' Asa it'll be a cinch."

"No."

"No one'd ever connect it with us. We'd ride south a day or two, ride up Coyote Wash, an' come up north again. No one t' see us."

"No."

"Don't'cha hate t' see all that Sheridan money goin' away forever? I don' unnerstan' you, by God, I don't! Gettin' soft in the head thinkin' 'bout that Parral gal?"

Sheridan turned slowly and stared at Sam.

Sam quickly mumbled, "Sorry, George."

Sheridan grunted. Sam went on, "Leave us take care of it. We'll leave the gal alone. Don' worry 'bout ol' Asa. He c'n shoot, he c'n ride, an' he c'n keep his mouth shut."

"You're a damn fool, Sam," Sheridan observed amicably. "An' I'll say why. I'm goin' down to Nacozari myself. *I'm* gonna make the deal with the general to buy him out. For that I'm gonna need money. Why should I carry money down with me an' worry 'bout bein' jumped for it all the way down there? Let Pearson

worry 'bout that. He'll take good care of it with the
Valdes boys. Damn good care—as good as I could
myself. An' when he gets down there, guess who'll be
there to greet 'im with both arms?''

Sam's mouth opened with a wide grin of admiration.

"We'll take the money off him with a polite thank
you,'' Sheridan said.

Sam said with enthusiasm, "*That's* the place to
bushwhack!''

"But first we gotta go see Mr. Watts an' maybe
spank 'im a bit to show 'im there's some life in the ol'
bastard still, eh? But I need 'im. So I'll spank 'im just a
li'l bit. There's lots of good information in 'im. I might
try t' buy some good Mex minin' property, or even
some Mex railroads. An' when I'm livin' down in
Sonora he'll be mighty useful to do my border business
for me. An' with someone up here I c'n trust runnin'
the old Big S—''

"You gonna *stay* in Sonora?''

"That de Parral gal made an offer to Pearson. He
don' look too interested to me. Or mebbe he is—but he
won't be able to do nothin' about it. I'll come by an' tip
my hat, an' say, 'Beggin' your pardon, ma'am, but I
hear tell you got a general an' his assistant to be
murdered in exchange for a hacienda.' An' she'll say,
'Why, yes, señor, that ees true.' An' I'll say, 'If you'll
step this way, ma'am, I'll make you a very dead
general.' ''

"But who's gonna run the Big S?''

"You, Sam.''

"Holy Moses!''

"But you gotta do as I say. Keep Eddie in line.
Smack 'im a bit if you have to. I'll come up twice

a year to look 'round. Better keep your nose clean, Sam.

"Now, when we get down to Nacozari, we gotta take possession very legal. Reason why is the U.S. Army'll be snoopin' 'round. I gotta get a signed receipt from the general. That's why we gotta handle Watts real gentle-like. He'll arrange all that. We'll have to hand over Pearson's cash to the general. We c'n take it back later, don' get your hackles up. That might take some doin'. He's no prairie flower, that one. He ain't gonna trust me; he ain't trustin' no one. He'll have his bodyguard everywhere he moves, day 'n' night. Nobody's gonna trust nobody, matter of fact. I don' want anyone jumpin' the gun or shootin' off his mouth down there. We'll need some very careful shootin'. That reminds me— what's Eddie doin'?"

"Tomcattin'."

"Get 'im. Tell 'im I got a job he'll like. Tell 'im it's somethin' he's been achin' to do for a long time. As long ago as the first time he ran across Mr. Pearson."

"He'll come a-runnin'."

Asa came out of the ranch house and walked unsteadily toward them. His walk was still energetic.

"That ol' buzzard stewed agin?" asked Sheridan. He was irritated. "He'll suck up all the loose rotgut in Nacozari."

"He mought be old," Sam said defensively, "but he's still a hard man with a gun."

They watched the dirty old man with his tobacco-stained white mustache as he wavered toward them. He wore a filthy buckskin vest and a turnip watch he had once stolen in a train holdup outside Holbrook. The watch had not worked for years. He always said he would get it fixed some day, and in the meantime the safest place for it was just where it was, across his belly at the end of a heavy gold watch chain.

"That soup-strainer of yours looks like a dead white mouse," said Sam.

"Shut up, y' danged fool," Asa said in a high-pitched whine. "This hand has tanned that backside of yours before an' it's itchin' t' do it agin, sheriff star or no."

"Wanna go fer a ride?"

"Nope!"

"Wanna stay here an' be a practice post for the kids to drop a riata over?"

"Me an' the pet goose," Asa said. "We don' mind. Better that than listen to your loose lips flip-flappin' all day. How come none o' you took out after that Mex gal? She's got lips rosy as a perch's gills, and her hair's as black as a hoss's tail. Twenny years ago I woulda clumb all over that Pearson feller to git at 'er. I ain't goin' *nowhere* with you."

"You're goin'," Sheridan said.

"No I ain't. You got no call to order *me* 'round, boy," he said savagely. "You take keer of us, you c'n give us orders. You're settin' up this Pearson like a king. You c'n go to hell!"

"Asa, it's all diff'rent now," Sam said soothingly.

"Shet up!"

"We're gonna take care of Pearson now. It's all fixed."

"You? You gotta go 'round with someone, kid, you ain't *never* alone, you or Eddie. You wanna go the gun route, you gotta be by yourself. But *you* gotta have someone always 'round holdin' your hand. It's gonna take *all* of us to bushwhack 'im, I got no more guts neither.'' He staggered back inside for another drink.

''He'll be all right when he's sobered up,'' Sheridan said calmly. He put his palms on his thighs and leaned forward.

''If you or *anyone* touches that de Parral gal,'' he said almost in a whisper, ''or even looks at 'er crossways, I'll make sure I'll be 'round to watch a buzzard pull his guts out of his asshole. Pass the word. An' get ready. We're leavin' in an hour.''

22

"Put away that star, you damn fool," Sheridan said. Sam muttered and took off his sheriff's star. Sheridan leaned forward from his saddle and tapped on Watts's big plate glass window.

Several vaqueros were lounging nearby gambling for ammunition with a pack of greasy cards.

Watts looked up from his desk. The day had been hot, and he was gently waving a fan back and forth.

Asa leaned back in his saddle and grinned. "He looks like his head just been took off," he chuckled. "Drained dryer'n a pint o' liquor among forty men. I'm ridin' down the street fer a drink."

"Don' get lost, you ol' fool!" said Sheridan.

Watts came out, still holding the fan. "Pleased to see you, George," he said. "Come in and set a while."

Sheridan looked at him without expression. He dismounted and tossed the reins to Eddie.

"Hi, Watts," Sam said. Watts nodded nervously.

Sheridan nodded toward the vaqueros. "Don' like their looks," he said. "Who the hell are they?"

"General's people. Town's crawlin' with 'em."

"Where's the army that chased him outa Mexico?"

"About ten miles east. And they're about ten miles inside Mexico too."

"How come?"

"The Mex army's got orders to stay plenty far away

from the border. President is lookin' for U. S. money to invest in railroads and industry, so he doesn't want to risk any incidents with U. S. citizens. These vaqueros just come in 'cause they felt like it, and there's no one here to chase 'em back. General can't control 'em all.'' Watts mopped his face with a handkerchief. "Hot, isn't it?"

"I ain't rode a couple hundred miles real hard t' talk 'bout weather."

"Come on inside," Watts said. "I plumb forgot my hospitality." Sheridan grunted and walked in. He sat down on Watts's desk and waved the fan gently as he watched Watts in silence.

Watts opened a cigar box and offered it. Sheridan smelled one, nodded, and shoved a handful into his pocket. He took another handful and gave them to Eddie. "I don' smoke," Eddie said.

"I know damn well you don' smoke," Sheridan said testily. "But I got no more room in my pockets." Eddie sullenly shoved them inside his shirt pocket. Watts struck a match and held the flame for Sheridan. His hand trembled slightly. Sheridan smiled and struck a match himself and held it beside Watts's match. Sheridan's hand was as steady as a granite boulder.

"Clean livin', Watts. Try it. An' another way I keep healthy—I trust myself. No one else."

"Don't blame you." Watts's match burned his fingers. He cursed and dropped it.

"A man ain't careful," Sheridan said, "he c'n burn hisself. Know what I mean?"

"Sure, sure."

"Mebbe you don', Watts. I read the letter you wrote Mr. Pearson." He began to unbuckle his gun belt.

"Pity God didn't put fur on some people so's you could shoot 'em at sight."

Watts stared with his mouth open. Eddie moved close to the desk and put his hand on his gun butt.

"I'm gonna tan your hide a bit," Sheridan said, amiably, "jus' to prove I'm gonna be around a bit longer. Stand up."

"Take it easy, now, Sheridan. I don't blame you for gettin' steamed up. The letter is a fake."

"Stand up!"

"I'm tellin' you, the letter is a fake!"

Sheridan heard someone walk into the office. Without turning around, he said, "Eddie, throw that feller out."

"For the last time, Sheridan, that letter was a fake!"

Eddie said, "I ain't throwin' this feller out."

"Do what I say!"

"He ain't no feller," Eddie said. "He looks like a general to me. He's got lots of men with 'im, too. You better turn around."

The general was leaning against the window with his arms folded across his chest. Outside, their faces pressed against the glass, were the vaqueros who had been playing for ammunition.

When he knew that Sheridan was looking at him he sauntered inside.

"That your private army?" Sheridan asked without preamble.

The general lifted an assenting palm.

"Señor Sheridan."

"Well?"

"Watts an' me, we write the letter. A good letter. No?"

Sheridan turned to Watts and said, "Beg your pardon."

23

Sheridan buckled on his belt again. Watts sank back in his chair with a sigh of relief.

The general said, "War is like ranching—there are good years, and there are bad years, no? Thees is a bad year."

"Yeah," Sheridan said, amused.

"I wan' to see thees Pearson fella again, Mr. Sheridan. Watts too. We wait. An' Sebastiano Valdes, I don' like him neither. I take care of heem, too. We been waitin' on the road, one week now, night an' day. We don' see 'im. Mebbe you see?"

"No. We rode so's we wouldn't catch up with 'im. We rode way east. We figgered we'd catch 'em 'round here."

"Three spiders," said the general, with a wide smile. "We wait for some leetle flies with money."

"Thought I'd remind you all," said Sheridan with a polite smile that was heavy with menace, "that it's *my* money the flies'll be carryin'. I don' wan' no arguments 'bout that."

"Your money?" the general asked with a tight smile.

"I bought his ranch, *amigo*. He's got that money with 'im. An' then he's got the money he cleared for hisself on our li'l deal."

"That ees *my* money."

"Not the way I see it," Watts said. "I didn't want to buy those carbines at the price he set on them."

182

"I figger it's *all* my money," Sheridan said heavily.

The general held out his hands, palms up. "The money, my friend, it belongs to the first one that gets it, no?"

"I don't like your attitude," Sheridan said. "If we're gonna fight over whose money it is before we ever see Pearson, we ain't *ever* gonna be friends, let alone run across 'im. So let's put it this way. If you get it first, it's yours, if we get it first, it's ours. If we all get it together, we split it."

"*Bueno, bueno!*"

Watts opened a drawer with a relieved grin and set a bottle of bourbon on the desk. He poured out two glasses. When Sheridan asked him why not three, he said he didn't drink. While Sheridan and the general drank, Watts asked, "What's the next step?"

Sheridan answered, "He's comin' in. Jus' how we don' know. He's smarter than us, as far as that's concerned, but he don' know he's walkin' into a bear trap. We'll jus' have to set here, with men prowlin' all 'round the country to scout for 'im. I'll think of some way to suck 'im in."

The general began to chuckle. He filled up his glass and began to shake with laughter.

"What's funny?" asked Sheridan.

"Don' worry," said the general. "I fix eet so Pearson comes in to Nacozari fast, fast! We sit here an' be cool an' make heem come to us, you see!"

24

Sebastiano and Slocum swam the river first, holding their carbines high in the air to keep them dry. When they were ashore Sebastiano placed his gnarled hand on Slocum's arm and said, ''Ay, *patrón*, we made it!''

He turned and waved the others across. When they were all together, Sebastiano rode ahead as scout. They had entered Mexico fifty miles upriver, came through unobserved, and had just re-entered Arizona to visit Sebastiano's home before they rode on to Nacozari. Now they were extra vigilant. They might run into the general any time.

Old Sebastiano Valdes became jittery with excitement. He had never been away from his wife so long, and, unable to control himself any longer, he let out several shrill coyote yelps as he and his nephews raced ahead.

He had no fears about leaving her alone. He was sure that the general would melt southwards into Mexico and reform his army again where they had originated, far to the south in Sonora. Very seldom did any Apaches pass near the ranch, and as for ordinary predators, she could easily handle anything with the Winchester that Sebastiano had taught her to shoot. She was a frontier woman.

Slocum turned and looked at Luisa. She was riding with her head down. He could not see her face but he knew that she was thinking that when she would come home to her hacienda there would be no such delight. He was stirred by her suppressed grief.

When Slocum and Luisa rode into the yard they saw the three Mexicans standing silently at their horses' heads, waist deep in weeds and wildflowers. Slocum instinctively knew that something bad had happened.

Horses had pawed and trampled the corn, crushing the little chickens to death. A log had been placed between the roof of the adobe house and a fork in the cottonwood. Señora Valdes and her two young grandsons hung from it. Two half-burned wagons stood in the corral, the fence of which was still smoldering. In the corral lay a dead burro. Two pots and a kettle hung from the low, fire-blackened branches of a little tree near the house. Underneath, a few cackling chickens huddled together.

Underneath the bodies of Señora Valdes and the children two shovels had been tossed. It was a message that Slocum knew meant very plainly that Sebastiano should be saved the trouble of looking for them.

Slocum hoped that Sebastiano would not notice that her murderers had ripped her gold earrings from her ears. But when the graves had been dug in the yard and the time had come to wrap her in a blanket Sebastiano saw.

As soon as the last shovelful had been thrown Sebastiano mounted. He had not said a word all this time. He jerked the horse's head toward Nacozari and jammed in his spurs. Never before had the old man treated a horse so savagely.

Slocum grabbed the reins. Sebastiano, white-faced, tried to pry the reins from Slocum's grip.

"*Adónde vas?*" shouted Slocum above the frightened whinnying of the horse. The horse was being spurred by its rider while at the same time Slocum had pulled its head sharply around to its withers. The puzzled and tortured horse thrashed in a circle to its left while Sebastiano, beginning to weep with frustrated rage, tried to jerk his reins out of Slocum's steel grip.

Sebastiano sobbed, "Let me go!"

Slocum shook his head.

"Por favor!"

"No, no! He wants you to ride into ambush, *viejo!* We will talk and make a plan. *Hombre,* listen!"

"I know these sons of whores! They don't wait for days in ambush! They're in town drinking and whoring! Let me go!"

"He's right!" said the older of the two boys, swallowing his tears. "Let him go, *patrón!*" He reached out and tried to pull his uncle's reins from Slocum's grip.

Suddenly old Valdes pulled his Colt and cocked it. *"Patrón Oígame! Por el amor de Dios!"*

Slocum looked at the cocked trigger and the plunging horse. He knew absolutely that if he did not let the reins go that Valdes, with the greatest regret, would shoot him. He let go.

The three men galloped toward the Rio Cuajaran.

"Oye, gringo."

He turned to Luisa. Her face was flushed. She had wiped away her tears and she spoke with icy formality.

"You're not going with them?"

"I'm not crazy."

"Listen. The spider made a web to catch the flies?" She pointed to the graves.

"Right."

"So you are clever if you don't walk into it?"

"Yes."

"But if the fly wants the spider as much as the spider

wants the fly? What then is the best way to find the spider?''

"Shake the web with both hands. But I want to be around a little longer than Sebastiano does.''

"Then you just stay here and wait till we come back and tell you what happened. *Adiós, querido*." She began riding toward the river.

"God damn it!" Slocum said. He would have preferred more time for planning, but her courage was forcing his hand. He cantered after her and pulled her reins till her horse halted.

"Take your hands off," she said softly.

"All you goddamn Mexicans!" Slocum said with exasperated admiration. "*You* wait here. I'll tell *you* what happened."

"And suppose the general sends someone here while you're in Mexico? The safest place is inside the web."

"Christ Almighty! Stop talkin' in riddles!"

"I want very, *very* much to see the general. And Pablo. Oh, I want to see Pablo very much. Please. So, *querido*, I come."

He hesitated. He looked at the grim yet lovely mouth set in its icy, savage calm.

"And then I will sleep without bad dreams. So kiss me.''

She kissed him fiercely, then she said, "I will stay if you kill them both."

"Yes."

"On the honor of your mother?"

"*Palabra de honor*," Slocum said. "Word of honor." He slapped her horse on the croup as he dug his spurs into his horse's flanks. Once across the Rio Cuajaran, he turned. She was looking at him. As Slocum rammed the dry carbine back into the saddle scabbard he turned and lifted a hand in farewell. She sat her horse and made no sign of recognition. Slocum turned again and rode into Mexico with his hand on his Colt's butt. Five minutes later he heard a drumming of hooves behind him. He spun around and waited tensely with his Colt out. But it was only Luisa.

All she said was, "I changed my mind. I ride with you all the way."

"I figured," Slocum said.

25

"You got a map of this country 'round here?" Sheridan asked. Watts nodded and pulled down a big wall map.

"Where are we?"

Watts pointed.

"All right. Where's ol' Valdes's place?"

"Out along this road."

"So they'd come along this road here, right?" asked Sheridan softly. "An' turn down this street here where we are right now?"

Watts nodded.

Sheridan went on, still speaking softly. "An' come down an' put their paws right smack in the middle of our bear trap an' *bang!*" He clapped his huge hands together as hard as he could. When Watts jumped he roared with laughter.

"All right. Any way they c'n ride outa town?"

Watts stared at the map. "There's an alley up the street a bit. Aside from that, they got to ride all the way back to this fork where they come into town. Or they can ride two hundred yards more and then cut into the chaparral."

"An' then?"

"That—that's it."

"Nervous?"

"A little. I tell you, gunfightin' ain't in my line."

"This ain't gunfightin'," Sheridan said contemptuously. "This is shootin' fish in a barrel. No call to git so excited. Gen'ral, you'll set 'bout six, seven men here—" Sheridan noticed but calmly disregarded the narrowing of the general's eyes at being given orders— "right where the road forks comin' down from the Rio Cuajaran. Then you—"

The general lifted a dirty forefinger and slowly wagged it back and forth. He leaned toward the street and listened. Satisfied, he leaned back in his chair and, grinning, pointed toward the street.

Pablo galloped up, slid off his panting horse, and jangled into Watts's office.

"Qué pasó?" demanded the general. Pablo bent forward and whispered into the general's right ear, grinning at Eddie.

"Ay, bueno!" said the general, clapping Pablo on his back in approval. Turning to Sheridan he said, "The flies are coming!"

"Haylo," Pablo said to Eddie, practicing his English. "How-do-you-do?" He had gotten over his habit of covering his mouth whenever he spoke.

"Pablo speak English vairy good," said the general.

"Sí, good!" Pablo said proudly.

Asa walked into the office. He sank into a chair with a groan of pleasure, saw the bottle of bourbon, heaved himself up again, took the bottle, sat down with it and a glass, and poured himself a full glass.

"We'll have to spot our men 'round," Sheridan said, looking at Asa with irritation. "I got five of 'em."

"Looks more like four," Watts said.

"He c'n hold his own, don' worry. Watts, how many men you got?"

Watts was pale. "Three."

"Plenny," the general said. "I got plenny men."

"How many?"

The general stared at Sheridan. *"Gringo,"* he said softly, "I tell you don' worry. I got plenny."

"Don' call me *gringo,* an' don' tell me not to worry. Don' tell me *nothin.'* I don' want no trouble with you before we finish with Pearson. How many carbines you got? I don' want no smart answers."

The general said nothing for a while. He stood up, sat down on Watts's desk. He put his palms on his greasy charro trousers with his elbows out. He rubbed his palms up and down slowly. Sheridan knew he was drying his palms in case he decided to make a fast draw. Pablo sprawled back against the window while he pushed a woman's gold earring on one finger after the other. The left hand finally wore the earring on the small finger while the right hand was still and placed against his right thigh, close to his gun butt.

"You like to geev orders, no?" The general broke the silence.

"I'm used to givin' orders, yeah," Sheridan said. "Shit, *hombre,* your army ain't worth shit these days." He lifted his eyebrows and stared briefly at Pablo. Eddie understood. He turned casually and faced Pablo, his right hand resting on his gun belt.

"I'm a gen'ral too," Sheridan. "How many guns you got here?"

The general did not think the boast was amusing. "I tell how many, what you do?" he asked. His face was hard.

"What'll I do?" Crissake, what the hell you think I want to know for? You're as hysterical as a schoolgirl."

The general dropped his hand to his gun. But Sheridan had his on his own gun butt a fraction of a second before. Asa chuckled and hugged himself with pleasure.

"Gentlemen, gentlemen!" Watts said, in agony.

"Evvabuddy kill evvabuddy in this yere office!" said Asa. "It'll make the funniest damn story. Evvabuddy in Arizona split their sides laughin' at us Sheridans. Now cut it out, damn it!" he roared, smashing his fist on the cigar box.

"You ruined my cigars, you old fool!" shouted Watts, as he cowered against the wall.

Asa went for his gun. The general roared with laughter as Sheridan hooked his right arm into Asa's bent right arm as the old man went for his Colt. Asa gave up in disgust. "You bunch o' sheep guts!" he shouted in rage.

"Where you goin', ol' man?" Sam demanded, blocking him.

"I'm headin' fer a drink straighter'n an Injun goin' to shit," said Asa. "Git outa my way."

"Looka here—" Sam began.

"I said *git!*" Asa's hand settled on his gun butt.

"Oh, for crissake," Eddie said wearily. "Let 'im git his drink. He's gittin' mean again."

"He ain't gonna sweeten up with rotgut, Eddie."

"Let 'im go, let 'im go," Sheridan said, disgusted. Sam reluctantly stepped aside.

"That's one less man we got," Watts said.

"The odds are still pretty good," Sheridan said. "Let me do the worryin'." A horse's hooves drummed suddenly down the dust-filled street. A vaquero leaned from the saddle and yelled through the door, "*Mi general!*"

The general walked quickly to the door. "*Sí?*"

"*Allí vienen cuatro hombres y una mujer, Doña de Parral!*"

"What's he sayin'?" asked Sam.

Sheridan said, "Four men and the de Parral gal are comin'."

The general motioned for the vaquero to take up a position across the street. The man dismounted, slapped the horse on the flank, and, as the horse trotted away, the man ran across the street and posted himself in an alley with a drawn gun.

"There goes my plan!" Sheridan said. "Scatter and use your common sense. If you got any, which I doubt." The men scattered. Some ran across the street, some clattered upstairs. Watts sank to his knees behind the desk.

"What the hell you gonna do, pray?" demanded Sheridan.

Watts opened his desk drawer and pulled out a Colt. "I want some protection, that's all." He slammed the drawer shut. "The desk is made of nice thick oak, and that's where I'm stayin'."

"It's gonna be fifteen to five—what the hell you 'fraid of? An' one of the five's a woman!" He laughed. "Come t' think 'bout it, Asa did say we was a bunch o' sheep guts."

"What the hell you talkin' about?" demanded the nervous, excited Watts. "They in sight yet?"

Sheridan walked calmly to the door. He looked outside. "Yeah. There they come. An' our Mr. Pearson, he's right out front." He looked at the men stationed everywhere where there was good shelter. "Y' know, Watts, I never bushwhacked no one. I just mought get ashamed of myself in a couple minutes."

Eddie was smiling to himself and moving his lips soundlessly. He kissed a cartridge and levered it into the firing chamber. Watts jumped nervously at the sudden, sharp click.

"Where they now?" he asked.

"Only a couple hundred yards to go, Watts. You'll know better when the firin' starts." He grinned at Watts's pale face.

"*Oye, hombres!*" called the general sharply from the roof. Three of his men looked up. He told them to sit on the sidewalk and pretend to be gambling.

"*Oye*, Sheridan," the general called softly.

"What you want?"

"The mice come for the cheese. No treecks with the money, *comprende?*"

When the riders were fifty feet from Watts's office the general yelled, "Fire!"

Luisa's horse shuddered and staggered. The men who had been told to gamble plunged wildly into the office and began firing. Slocum grabbed for the reins of Luisa's horse but the horse dropped, pinning her underneath. One of Valdes's nephews fell dead with three bullets in his back. His horse trotted off, dragging the dead man by a spur still jammed in the stirrup. One of the general's men who had run into Watts's office from the street raced outside, pulled the dead man's carbine from his dead grip, and waved it aloft triumphantly. Slocum shot him in the head. He fell, writhing in agony.

Sheridan heard the general clattering down the stairs. Sebastiano had been shot in the lower jaw by the heavy bullet. Half the jaw had been blown away. The bullet went ranging up through his brain, making an exit hole as big as a silver dollar. He was still alive. His feet jerked spasmodically.

Slocum flung himself from his horse. Together with Ricardo Valdes he plunged into a chili parlor. The woman cook was cringing in a corner next to the stove and screaming. Slocum ran behind the counter and grabbed her arm. She pulled away and screamed louder. He jerked hard and she fell flat on the floor, closed her eyes as tightly as she could, and went on screaming.

"Shut up and don't move!" Slocum ordered in Spanish. She subsided and lay still. Holes appeared in the windows and in the front of the counter. A vinegar bottle exploded just above him.

"Don't move!" Slocum called out to Luisa. She understood and lay motionless.

"Ricardo! Someone's up in that second-story window. See if you can—"

"*Patrón*," Ricardo said apologetically.

Slocum turned. Ricardo's right shoulder blade had been broken. Blood dripped out of the end of his sleeve. Slocum ripped up a dirty dish towel and made a sling. He balled up another towel and shoved it inside Ricardo's shirt to stop the flow of blood. Volley after volley poured into the place. A pot of sauce burst above the cook and sprayed her with what she thought was blood. Her screams settled into a monotone. Occasionally some powdery white dust drifted down on them as a bullet dislodged some of the dried clay in the adobe wall.

Sheridan watched. He had not fired once.

Pablo watched the dying Sebastiano draw up his right leg and kick erratically like a frog. His eyes were wide open, but he was unconscious.

"*Oye, gringo!*" Pablo called out. "Valdes, he wan' die but he can't die nohow!" He began crawling in the dust toward Luisa, still pinned under the weight of her dead horse. Her carbine had been knocked out of her hands by the fall and lay just out of her reach. As she saw Pablo edging toward her she clawed desperately for the carbine, but she could not reach it. Pablo reached the Winchester and pushed it behind him with a triumphant grin. Her fingers clawed at the dust in helpless anger. He was only three feet from her. He pulled out his Colt and cocked it and was bringing it down to bear on her face when Slocum got in a snap shot which smashed the Colt's cylinder. Pablo shook his tingling hand and grinned, then pressed his body flat. His broken teeth in the smiling mouth looked like a wolf's.

He reached out and grabbed one of her long black braids. *"Buenas tardes, Doña Luisa,"* he said, and jerked her head violently around until it was wrenched against her right shoulder. She thrashed about, trying frantically to free herself from his dirty hand. His one good eye stared at her; the other socket was still red and raw. Her hand clawed at the dust. Suddenly she picked up a handful of the dust and threw it in his face. He recoiled, sneezing and coughing; his one good eye was temporarily blinded. He rubbed his eye and gasped, *"Espere poquito, puta!* Wait a second, you whore!" He held on to her hair.

A Colt with its butt studded with tiny silver symbols skidded to a halt against her arm. She grabbed it and cocked it. Pablo shook his head once more, pulled his knife, and opened his still-tearing eye. For the first time he saw the Colt. He lifted his knife and she fired.

The heavy bullet knocked him to one side. He struggled to his knees and looked down. The bullet had gone through his chest. He lifted the knife again and she fired three times, sobbing and cursing him with each shot. The impact knocked him on his back. Once more he struggled to his knees. She shot twice more, but missed because her hand was shaking. Pablo grinned and raised the knife as high as he could, holding his left palm flat against his chest to stem the flow of blood. Then he plunged it down as hard as he could. Slocum fired. The knife dropped from Pablo's shattered right wrist, and Pablo died.

Sheridan threw away his cigar. "Damn it," he said softly, "an' I had it all figgered out so nice." He stepped out into the street with the carbine under his arm. The firing slowed, then stopped as the puzzled men watched him.

He walked across the street to her horse. She stared upward at him while she pointed the Colt at him. "I c'n count pretty good, *señorita*," he said dryly. "You done fired it six times. That's all she holds." He put down the Winchester, put his shoulder against the dead horse, and shoved. His great strength moved it easily. The carcass slid away. "Your leg busted?" She shook her head.

He bent down and picked up Sebastiano Valdes's Colt from its holster. He lifted the old man's right eyelid and let it drop. He grunted. He stood up and took Luisa's arm and led her to the restaurant. Slocum raised his carbine as they came in.

"What am I supposed to do?" Slocum asked. "Surrender? You're covered, Sheridan."

"Put it down, boy." He tossed the Colt to Slocum, who caught it in mid-air. "Git down flat," Sheridan told Luisa. "Do it *fast*. They'll be catchin' on right soon."

Slocum stared at him, puzzled. "You come to talk?" he demanded.

"Hell, no. Jus' evenin' out the odds."

"Why?"

"Jus' say it's more fun for me thataway." He grinned and jerked his head toward the men outside. "They can't figger it out yet, but they will, right soon. What's the matter, boy?"

"I can't figure *you* out."

"Allus one step ahead of the crowd. Figger out what the smartest one will do next—an' then go one more step ahead."

"What advantage you got comin' here? Now you got everyone out there mad at you."

"It was too easy out there. I ain't had so much fun in years as I figger t' have with you mighty soon. Now you an' the lady sit back an' relax while my relatives start their hollerin'."

"Still can't figure you."

"Allus liked a man who took big chances. Now *I'm* takin' 'em. I feel fine! Now you jus' pile up your cartridges an' let's get ready."

As if on schedule Eddie called out from behind his corner, "Hey, Sam!"

"Yeah?"

"Y' see the son of a bitch skip his Colt to that gal?"

"I seen it. He's gone crazy. What the hell's he doin' in there?"

"I thought he went in to talk, an' I bet they're keepin' him in there till they make their getaway."

"What the hell did he give 'er the Colt fer?"

"To show he wanted to be friends. He's tricky—hey, George, you all right?"

Sheridan grinned as he lay flat on his back behind the counter.

"Yeah, I'm fine!" he bellowed.

"They got a gun in his back," Sam said.

"Listen, Sam," Eddie said, dropping his voice, "if George gets kilt—if he gets killed accidental—"

"Yeah, I know! They'll kill 'im if we don' let 'em get away!"

Eddie looked at him contemptuously.

"If he gits kilt," he said coldly, "then *we* inherit."

"Gits kilt?"

Eddie said nothing.

"Jeez," Sam said, comprehending at last. "Accidental."

"Yeah. Real accidental, you fat son of a bitch."

"You're the boy who does the fancy shootin'. You better do the best accidental shootin' of your life, kid."

"You mean shoot my own cousin?" Eddie said dryly.

"I'm shocked, kid."

"Don't be, Sam."

"Jus' make that shot that'll get us a million and a half acres, eleven thousand head, fifteen artesian wells, three hundred and fifty miles o' bobwire fences, an' we'll have the Governor of the Territory lickin' our hands ev'ry time we go visitin' 'im to give orders. Belly down there like an ol' coon, Eddie, an' git to work."

"An' the second shot'll be for Pearson. That's the one I really been waitin' to squeeze off."

Sheridan said thoughtfully, "Y' know 'bout Eddie an' his shootin'?"

"Yep," Slocum replied.

"Gimme your hat."

Sheridan took it and pushed it gently above the counter edge. Eddie fired and blew a lamp chimney a foot away to bits.

"He ain't strikin' an empty hook, that boy ain't. That's his way of tellin' us to go to hell. We gotta suck that boy out. He's too smart for that hat trick. He needs live bait."

He turned and asked Luisa for his inlaid Colt. She

slid it along the floor. He reloaded it. "O.K.," he said. "Git ready."

Slocum nodded. He crouched, prepared to stand up and shoot.

Sheridan poked his Colt around the edge of the counter. Eddie's eyes widened as he recognized both the gun and his uncle's gold wedding band. He fired instantly. Slocum stood up and fired as Eddie was busy ejecting the shell. Eddie had worked the lever so fast that when the bullet struck him he was pulling the trigger. But the impact of the slug in his stomach made the shot go wild. He lurched sideways from behind the pillar.

He walked very slowly along the sidewalk, then sat down on it. Then he got up, staggered a few paces, and leaned against a wall. He held on to the window sill for a few seconds with his back to the street. Then he fell backward with his wide-open eyes staring at the sky.

"Fair exchange," said Sheridan. He held up his right hand. Eddie had shot off his forefinger. He wrapped a towel around it.

The general had commandeered a wagon and built a barricade on it out of full sacks of corn meal. Several men were behind the sacks, their carbines poking out at the ready. As the wagon rattled by the men fired into the restaurant at full volume. From their superior height they could easily rake the restaurant.

The wagon turned around and prepared to make another pass. Slocum stood up while Sheridan fired at Sam and the others to make them keep their heads down; as the wagon neared, Slocum shot the horses. They went down, squealing and thrashing. One by one he shot the men. After the third man was shot, the others broke and ran. Sheridan ran to the door and pegged a shot after them. A bullet seared his face.

Across the street, Sam frantically worked the lever for his next shot.

Sheridan shot first. Sam screamed like a rabbit and, clutching his throat, fell to his knees and choked. He fell face down into the dust.

The general, Slocum, and Sheridan all fired simultaneously. The general, who had run from the wagon and had by now gained the roof across the street, looked surprised. He straightened up from a half-crouch. He looked down at his chest, where two red blotches were beginning to widen. He looked confused, as if a complicated puzzle in a difficult language had just been asked. He stared next at Sheridan, and then began to cross himself. Before he could finish his heart stopped. He fell backward, but one leg slipped over the edge and hung there, swinging slowly back and forth. The curved silver pesos on his charro trousers flashed as the oscillations of the general's dead leg caught the late-afternoon sun.

Sheridan felt a dull thud in his left shoulder blade and then a sharp pain near his heart. At first he thought that Slocum had struck him accidentally with his carbine barrel as he whipped the Winchester around to face the general on the roof, but it was not until he felt blood trickling down his back that he realized he had been hit. It seemed to him that his spine had turned to jelly. He felt his knees giving way under him. There was no pain, only a cool interest in what was happening to him. The startled expression on Slocum's face, followed by concern, amused him. His head dropped onto his chest and he fell. He felt drowsy and very relaxed. He opened his eyes and looked up at the dirty ceiling.

Slocum and Luisa were staring down at him. From the other end of the town came the sound of a Mexican army bugler. Then the crashing boom of a cannon. Slocum looked out warily. The general's men had all fled before the advancing federal army.

Sheridan thought wryly, *I'm out of luck today*. Aloud he said, "We both got 'im. Even with my bum hand I take half the credit." He was amused once more by Slocum's puzzled look.

Slocum bent down and said, "I can't hear you."

Then George Sheridan knew he was going to die. "All right," he shouted, "y' better git out fast." From Slocum's still-puzzled face Sheridan knew his voice was too weak. He said as distinctly as he could, "Too many people'll start askin' stupid questions."

"Sheridan—"

"Lemme finish! Hard to hear you. Not much time. Hit the river runnin'. Take my Colt an' give it to your first son to teeth on. Y' hear, damn it? Take it while I c'n still see."

Slocum took it.

"You were too smart fer yourself an' too smart fer me. But you're a man to ride the river with! Wish we coulda bin partners thirty years ago, we coulda gone far together—" Sheridan's last thought was that Slocum had not heard a word. He died.

26

Watts cautiously lifted his head as Slocum and Luisa galloped down the street past the admiring stares of the federal army officers. He walked down the street and looked into the restaurant. The woman cook was still whimpering in a shrill monotone as she looked at the wreckage.

"Shut up!" Watts said, exasperated.

Four troopers on the roof across the street were lowering the general's body. Watts walked shakily into the *pulqueria*.

Sitting alone at the dark bar was old Asa. He was drunk. "Where's my hoss?" he demanded.

"Dunno," said Watts.

"Don' tell me some greasy stinkin' 'pache done stole 'im! They like hosses better'n beef."

Watts watched a cavalry squad survey the dead horses still in their traces.

"The dirty buggers et my saddle hoss oncet," Asa went on. "A crackerjack! While they was plenny cattle 'round." He got up and said to the bartender, who did not understand English, "You seen anythin' o' my hoss?" The man shook his head and shrugged his shoulders, smiling.

Asa clung to the bar in speechless fury. It was then Watts suddenly realized that Asa had been so drunk that he did not know what had just happened to all his relatives.

Watts said to the bartender, "*Dame una bebida. Una bebida grande.* A big drink. A *big* drink."

The bartender looked at him surprised. "*Pero usted no bebe, Señor!* You don't drink!"

"I do now!"

He drank it in one gulp. "For crissake," he muttered to himself, "look who owns the Sheridan ranch!"

Asa staggered out into the sun. "Kill the sumbitch who stole my hoss," he mumbled. He walked a few steps, stumbled, and fell into the bloody dust. "That hoss was a crackerjack," he mumbled with his mouth pressed into the bloody dust where Sam had just died. "A crackerjack." He passed out.

Watts turned back to the bartender. "*Un otro,*" he said in awe. "Another one."